"I'll show you mine, if you show me yours..."

"Come again?" Carly asked.

Matt's gray eyes darkened and the playfulness that had been there a moment ago turned into something smoky. He bent in to narrow the gap between them, stoking her desire.

"The rest of your answers. You've forgotten that I saw a couple of them already." He dropped his eyes to her lips. "I don't think you were toying with the survey when you completed the section about sex.... I think you were telling the truth."

Carly dug her fingers into her office chair. "It's just a silly questionnaire."

The corners of his mouth cocked into a smile. "I don't think there's anything silly about this heat between us. I think we might do ourselves justice by seeing where it goes."

She really should object, knowing what she knew about the fudged survey. But with Matt, she didn't want to be decent. She wanted to be delightfully bad. Because no matter how wrong he was about the results, she hadn't lied on every question.

He was right. When it came to sex, she and Matt were a perfect match....

Dear Reader,

I've often seen those matchmaking commercials on TV. You know, the ones with those happy couples who look perfect for each other dancing to the promise of long-lasting love? The romantic in me smiles every time I see all those happily-ever-afters packed into one thirty-second spot.

The writer in me insisted there was a juicy story in there somewhere. For an angle, I knew it had to involve cheating of some sort. I wanted my heroine to lie through her teeth on the survey, then get stuck being matched to the wrong guy. Ideally, he'd be someone she knew. Even more perfect, someone she absolutely hated. Oh, and in the midst of all that, she'd be forced to pretend to be his soul mate. After all, what's interesting about cheating if it doesn't get a girl into trouble? So once the details were in place, I ended up with a story that was a total blast to write.

In the following pages Carly Abrams is about to discover that, while you might be able to boil matchmaking down to a science, true love is nothing short of magic.

Happy reading!

Lori Borrill

PUTTING IT TO THE TEST

Lori Borrill

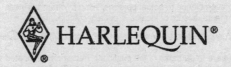

HARLEQUIN®

TORONTO • NEW YORK • LONDON
AMSTERDAM • PARIS • SYDNEY • HAMBURG
STOCKHOLM • ATHENS • TOKYO • MILAN • MADRID
PRAGUE • WARSAW • BUDAPEST • AUCKLAND

ISBN-13: 978-0-373-79396-9
ISBN-10: 0-373-79396-0

PUTTING IT TO THE TEST

Copyright © 2008 by Lori Borrill.

This edition published by arrangement with Harlequin Books S.A.

® and TM are trademarks of the publisher. Trademarks indicated with ® are registered in the United States Patent and Trademark Office, the Canadian Trade Marks Office and in other countries.

www.eHarlequin.com

Printed in U.S.A.

ABOUT THE AUTHOR

An Oregon native, Lori Borrill moved to the Bay Area just out of high school and has been a transplanted Californian ever since. Her weekdays are spent at the insurance company where she's been employed for over twenty years, and she credits her writing career to the unending help and support she receives from her husband and real-life hero. When not sitting in front of a computer, she can usually be found at the Little League fields playing proud parent to their son, Tom. She'd love to hear from readers and can be reached through her Web site at www.LoriBorrill.com, or via mail addressed to Harlequin Enterprises, Ltd., 225 Duncan Mill Road, Toronto, Ontario M3B 3K9, Canada.

Books by Lori Borrill
HARLEQUIN BLAZE
308—PRIVATE CONFESSIONS
344—UNDERNEATH IT ALL

To the many friends and coworkers at the office who have been a source of support and encouragement from the very start. You make the daily grind worth showing up for!

For Al and Tommy.

1

I TEND TO BE conservative when it comes to sex.

Carly Abrams studied the survey option, wondering if she should answer based on her actual sex life or the one she really wanted. So far in her twenty-six years she hadn't exactly pushed any sexual boundaries. But that wasn't *her* fault. She simply hadn't connected with any adventurous men. Give her the right partner with the right moves at the right time, and a very kinky side of Carly Abrams could make a flashing debut. The fact that it hadn't happened yet shouldn't be held against her, should it?

"No, it shouldn't," she muttered, then clicked the box titled *Disagree*. She briefly paused over *Strongly Disagree*, thinking if she was making a sexual admission, she might as well go all the way, but decided to leave it be. It was pointless to over-analyze the questions. Though this was a matchmaking survey, she wouldn't be finding any soul mates on the design team at Hall Technologies. This was only an exercise to select the two Web designers who would be assigned to the company's latest client, Singles Inc., an online matchmaking and dating service in need of a fresh new Web site.

A number of firms had vied for the account, Singles Inc. attracting some of the biggest names in advertising and Web design. But though Hall Technologies was no leader in the

industry, Brayton Hall had landed the account with his uncon-
ventional style and his concepts about becoming one with the
client, which in this case included using the client's compatibility survey to select the project's design team.

Everyone who wanted a shot at the job had to fill it out,
though employees had the option of skipping any questions
they felt uncomfortable answering.

Like this next one.

*When it comes to sex, nothing's too far out for me. Bring
on the toys, tie me up and invite a friend to join us. "The
wilder, the better" is my motto.*

Well, if she were looking to connect with adventurous
men, this would certainly be the way to do it.

Fidgeting with the hem of her canary-yellow tunic, she
stared at the screen and smiled. Wouldn't Mr. Hall keel over
if she *strongly agreed* to that statement? Not that she expected
him to read the answers. They'd made a big deal out of men-
tioning that Singles Inc. would tally the results and that no one
at Hall Technologies would be privy to detailed information.

Still, if he did, it would be a riot. Ms. Sally Sunshine, as
she was often regarded, coming out of her tidy closet to reveal
a fetish for bondage, dildos and threesomes. Just the image
of Mr. Hall's reaction had her clicking *Strongly Agree* for fun
and tempting herself to leave it that way. Of course, it
wouldn't be true. Though toys and bondage might have raided
her fantasies, she couldn't quite make the jump into threesomes—and she could hardly cop to the label of "wild" if
she'd never even broached "moderate."

Yet she couldn't help staring at her answer as if she were
trying the idea on for size.

"When it comes to sex, nothing's too—"

The low, sultry voice over her shoulder caused her to jump and slap a hand to the screen.

Please don't let that be who she thought it was.

"—far out for me."

Oh, heck. It was. Matt Jacobs, the bane of her existence, the thorn in her professional side. *The star of your sexual fantasies.*

Oh, no. Scratch that last errant thought. Matt Jacobs was most definitely *not* her sexual fantasy. In fact, the only fantasy she had of Matt involved him making a fool out of himself in front of as many people as possible, getting fired, packing up his belongings and tripping over the threshold on his way out the door.

Yeah, now there's a fantasy to get hot about.

Frowning, she tossed over her shoulder, "Do you mind?" But instead of backing off, he moved in closer and chuckled lightheartedly, filling her space with the sound of his voice and sending a tingle through her veins that exposed that last thought as a lie.

Okay, so maybe she was still harboring a few remnants of the crush she'd developed two years ago, back when he'd first swaggered into Hall Technologies from their rival design firm, Web Tactics. He'd been a noted acquisition for Hall, and Carly, as the lead Web programmer, had been sold on his arrival. The two were supposed to have formed a team, working together to tackle the biggest projects that came through the door. But that was before he waltzed in and told management he could do it alone, knocking her off their first project and snagging every other good account that had come in since.

That she'd actually held a torch for the man embarrassed her, that the torch still hadn't gone out dismayed her. And that he'd picked this precise moment to pay her a visit took the cake entirely. This could go down as a banner moment in Carly Abrams's life if he'd actually seen her answer to the survey question. It was bad enough he'd rejected her; now only the ninth-grade belching incident could top the humiliation of Matt Jacobs thinking she was into extreme kinky sex.

With her right hand still covering the screen, she awkwardly reached for the mouse with her left, trying in a nonchalant way to minimize the window. Instead it came off looking like some bizarre game of computer-monitor Twister.

"I never would have pegged you as a threesome kinda gal," Matt whispered into her ear, cluing her in to the fact that he had, indeed, read the answer.

Heat swarmed her cheeks. The ninth-grade belching incident officially fell to number two on the list. Matt Jacobs— her darkest professional foe, reluctant personal heartthrob— now thought she was some kind of closet porn queen.

Letting her hands fall to her sides, she jutted her chin and turned toward Matt, putting up her best front despite the fact that her eyes couldn't quite reach his.

"What can I do for you, Matt?"

There. Perfectly calm and cool. She wasn't about to justify his comment with an answer. And as long as she didn't let her eyes wander above his knees, she was almost guaranteed not to swallow her tongue.

He shifted and leaned against her desktop, and a wisp of something burly swept across her nose, drugging her senses with the scent of rugged man.

Okay, so she could hold her breath, too. No problem.

But as she held the air in her lungs, licked some moisture onto her lips and tried to keep her eyes diverted from that hard, sinewy chest, she feared how stupid she probably looked.

Inwardly she groaned. Why did she always turn into an idiot around this man? It killed her, this effect he had on her. He was *so* not deserving of her affections, but to this day her brain hadn't managed to convince the rest of her body of that little fact. Even at this very moment her nipples had gone erect, as if to sit up proper and make a good impression. Didn't they know he needed to be shunned?

"Hmm, what you can do for me," he said. "Given what I know now, several things come to mind."

Her jaw dropped and she flicked her gaze to his in time to catch his wink. Those devilish gray eyes bored into her, taunting her with his knowing glare, and it suddenly occurred to her just how badly this could end up. He had a look that said he was one Sharpie short of scribbling *For a good time call...* in all the restrooms, and in a frantic move to correct him she blurted, "I lied."

He blinked. "You what?"

"The survey. My answer. It's not true."

He held his big hands up in truce. "Hey, your private life is none of my business."

Okay, so he could have said that with slightly less conviction. Her private life definitely wasn't his business, but he didn't have to express his disinterest so convincingly.

Crossing her arms over her chest to conceal her traitorous breasts, she pronounced, "Well, it's not. I only put that answer there to toy with Mr. Hall."

Matt stood for a moment and stared.

"You what?"

"It's a joke. Or a lesson, depending on how you look at it. Hall said the surveys were confidential, but just in case he takes a peek at our answers, I decided to leave him a shocker."

Matt blinked, then blinked again, then threw his head back and laughed. "I didn't know you had it in you."

"Had what?"

"A joke. That's priceless."

Her jaw dropped for the second time. What was worse—him thinking her a pervert or him thinking her humorless?

"I happen to be very funny," she defended, causing him to drown out his chuckle with a cough.

"I'm sure you are," he said, but his tone said otherwise.

Rising to her feet, she clasped her hands to her hips and called over the cubicle wall to their coworker, Neil.

"Neil, I'm funny, aren't I?"

"You're hysterical," Neil agreed, though even his response sounded like a nagged husband just trying to keep peace in the family.

Lowering back to her chair, she told herself not to let it bother her. Matt was only trying to push her buttons, probably bent over the fact that the Singles Inc. account wasn't being handed to him on a platter like all the other top projects. In fact, now that she thought about it, the whole puzzle fit.

Since when had he ever left his corner of the floor to fraternize with the other designers? His desk was right outside the executive suite, which allowed him to continually buddy up to the bosses without having to cross paths with anyone else. Yet today he'd decided to stop by. And why? Because management had duped him on this latest assignment. Not only were they insisting a man and a woman work together on this one—Singles Inc. wanting to assure the new site appealed to both sexes—but to get the project Matt would have to show some sort of compatibility with a woman on the team.

And to match up with a woman he'd have to bother getting to know one.

Ha, she thought. Mr. High and Mighty didn't have a chance, and he knew it. So instead of filling out the survey and taking his chances, like everyone else, he was out trolling to compare answers. Why else would he have made reading her computer screen his first order of business?

Giving him a glare she hoped looked evil, she asked, "Why are you here?"

His bemused smile said her evil glare was about as threatening as a cream puff.

"Your *Ultimate HTML Guide*. I'd like to borrow it, if you don't mind. I took mine home and forgot to bring it back."

She poked her cheek with her tongue. "Are you sure about that?"

"Come again?"

"This must kill you, having to compete for a spot on the Singles Inc. project like everyone else."

"It's not a competition. It's about compatibility."

"Exactly, and it's probably only now occurred to you that you don't know a thing about the staff. Your odds of striking the highest match with anyone are slim at best."

He folded his arms across his chest and frowned, a stance that made him look deliciously menacing, and Carly had to will away a half dozen inopportune thoughts. The man was handsome to distraction, the kind of sexual magnet that jerked heads and caused women to walk into walls.

Tall, with a strong, square jaw, Matt Jacobs was about as close as they came to physical perfection, and no matter how badly Carly wanted to ignore him, she couldn't deny her attraction. He was the epitome of her ideal sex toy, dark and serious, strong and silent, yet still capable of flashing a grin that could turn the most pent-up woman into mush.

A layer of stubble hardened what might otherwise be a too-pretty face. He kept his dark, wavy hair cut just below the ears—short enough for the workplace but long enough to sink your fingers in—and when he smiled, a faint dimple sank into one cheek, softening those hard lines and warming everything around him.

His silver eyes had a habit of revealing his thoughts—this particular one screaming loud and clear annoyance—but despite his bone-melting nearness and disgruntled glare, Carly worked hard to keep the upper hand. This was the first time she'd ever confronted him with her opinion, and she wouldn't let a little temptation to fondle those biceps stop the momentum.

He stared at her for a moment, then feigned looking aghast. "You think I'm here to compare answers with you?"

"This would be the first major project you're not part of. Are you trying to tell me you'd leave the results up to fate?" Shaking her head, she huffed. "No way."

He looked at her as though she were insane, but she suspected it was a cover, that underneath the facade he was mortified she'd read him so easily.

"I'll just borrow your book now and go, if you don't mind," he said, reaching over her shoulder and pulling the manual from her overhead shelf.

She pushed back a smirk. "Keep it as long as you'd like."

And when he turned and left her cubicle, she smiled with satisfaction. Finally, after spending two years being backstage to Matt Jacobs, she was about to shine.

Granted, she wasn't guaranteed a spot on the team any more than he was. However, the simple fact that the Singles

Inc. account would be handed out based on something other than Matt's ability to suck up to the boss left her feeling that justice had rightfully returned to Brayton Hall Technologies.

And if, by some chance, she got the project over Matt, well, that would be the ultimate icing on the cake.

"WHY DO I LET HER get to me?"

Matt picked up the plastic bottle of ketchup, squeezed it over his fries, then passed it to his coworker, Adam, his closest friend at Hall Technologies.

The two men had connected last year when Adam discovered Matt had played AA ball for the Anaheim Nationals. Since the center of Adam's life was his men's softball team, he'd been itching to sign Matt up ever since learning of his past. Unfortunately for Adam, Matt wasn't about to step back into a dugout, and though Adam rechecked that status on a regular basis, he'd learned to accept Matt as nothing more than a lunch companion.

Their normal routine involved ducking out for deli sandwiches they brought back to their desks, using the quick stroll around the corner to stretch their legs and talk about sports. Matt's encounter with Carly this morning had him suggesting they dine out, and "burgers at Quimbly's," a nearby fifties-style diner, was all Adam needed to hear to agree.

"Because she's hot," Adam said. He squeezed a dollop of ketchup on his bacon cheeseburger and set the red plastic bottle back in the caddy next to its yellow-mustard mate.

Matt shook his head. "Lots of women are hot and none of them drive me crazy. Carly Abrams drives me crazy."

"They always say love exists on the edge of insanity."

Ignoring the comment—because he refused to grace that

stupidity with an answer—he pointed a crinkle-cut fry toward Adam. "She actually thought I'd come over to her desk to look at her answers to the survey." Scoffing, he added, "That is one twisted woman."

Though, granted, he had looked at her answers. Not just the one about being into wild, kinky sex but the one before it, as well, the one that said she was most definitely *not* conservative in bed. He genuinely hadn't come over prying for info on her survey, but he couldn't deny what he'd seen haunted him.

And the more he thought about it, the less he believed her story about toying with Old Man Hall. It was a nice try, but Matt couldn't shake the suspicion that Carly Abrams really did have a wild side in bed.

And he'd been semierect ever since.

"You have to admit, this is the first time you weren't given the big project," Adam said. "There have been rumblings over how you're dealing with that."

"I couldn't care less about Singles Inc. I've already spent two years proving myself to Hall. I don't need another big project to showcase my abilities."

And it was true. Matt hadn't come to Hall Technologies just to do more Web design. He'd come to learn the ropes from Brayton Hall, the man who was about to blow the lid off the traditional Web-design and electronic-advertising firms. Hall had spent two decades at IBM, being in on the ground floor of Internet technology back when the public barely knew what a dot-com was. He'd learned the rules from one of the industry leaders, then set out on his own to break them.

With the larger firms building corporate structures that turned them into slow-moving barges, Hall Technologies stayed nimble, hiring some of the brightest independent Web designers, who were accustomed to coming up with innovative ideas and delivering them fast. To the big players they were barely a blip on the radar, but Matt knew that was all about to change and he had every intention of being the guy to Hall's right when it happened.

"Not when there's a management position hitting the rumor mill, huh, pal?" Adam asked.

Matt was about to take a bite of his double cheeseburger when he stopped. "You heard about that?"

"Word's slowly getting around. I don't know how much truth there is to it, but we've got over a dozen designers in the department and the company keeps growing. Hiring another manager seems to fit."

"So what have you heard?"

Adam casually glanced around the room, making sure people with the wrong ears hadn't stepped into the restaurant, before answering.

"Only that he's looking to start up a specialized project team. Hall wants to go after some of the bigger clients and he's got ideas on how to do that without turning into another corporate slug. What those ideas are, I don't know, but I've heard he wants someone to take the lead on it so he can continue to focus on acquisitions."

"Yeah," Matt said. "That's what I heard, too." And the thought left him salivating. This was exactly the kind of thing he'd been waiting for, the precise reason he'd left his cushy job to prove himself all over again to Brayton Hall. The man was brilliant, and Matt wanted to be the recipient of that wisdom to someday maybe make partner or rival Hall with his own design firm.

Either way, it was a win-win situation, and instead of bothering himself with Singles Inc., he'd rather sniff out what he had to do to land that new position.

And when he got it, he'd be glad nothing had ever come of him and Carly. Despite her disdain for him, she was one of the sharpest minds at Hall Technologies. If Matt was to land this job, she'd be the first one he'd ask for. Granted, there was a chance she'd laugh in his face at the offer. He knew she'd resented him since the day he'd been hired, and his visit to her cube this morning had been yet another attempt on his part to chat it up and maybe broach a truce.

But, as always, he'd opened his mouth, said the wrong thing and started the downward spiral that only solidified her contempt for the ground he walked on. He hadn't meant to make the crack about the survey. He'd just seen her answers, turned hard as a rock and blurted out the first thing that popped into his mind—that her answer couldn't be true.

Because he needed it not to be true.

If he did get to assemble this new team, and Carly was on it... Well, he'd already been hot enough under the collar when it came to her without believing she had a wild side when it came to sex.

Knowledge like that, if proven true, could likely kill him.

"And I take it you're the man for the job?" Adam asked.

"I'd like to think so. Any rumors where *that's* concerned?"

"Only speculation. There isn't anyone in Programming or Sales with the expertise to handle it, so most people are assuming they'd pick someone from our unit, most likely you or Carly."

He raised a brow. "Carly?"

Adam shrugged. "She's been here from the start, had been the number one designer before you came along. And she's a team player, a favorite among the programmers and business-development execs. She's got the affection of everyone on staff, so in that respect," he said, tipping his glass toward Matt, "I'd consider her a contender if I were you."

Matt dismissed Adam's enthusiasm but didn't let the sentiment show on his face. Sure, everything he'd said about Carly was true, but since Matt had come on board, Hall had practically been grooming him for a spot on the management team. All signs pointed to the idea that *she* would be working for *him* someday, not the other way around, but he didn't need to further strain his relationship with her by spreading that notion around.

So he lied.

"Yeah, I suppose Carly would be another viable candidate." Then, getting back to his meal, he added, "I guess we'll have to see how things pan out."

2

"DO YOU THINK I'm funny?"

Carly posed the question to her friend, Bev, as they stepped out of the offices of Hall Technologies and into the bright midday sunshine. For almost a year now the two women had been spending their lunch hours power walking through the industrial park that housed Hall Technologies and several other high-tech firms just north of San Francisco. That was, of course, unless the weather was bad or one of them was up against a deadline. Or if they had errands to run or there was a sale at Paulson's. And never on Fridays, when the Sub Shack ran their two-for-one lunch special.

In truth, today was the first time in two weeks they'd sufficiently run out of excuses and opted for the walk.

"What do you mean? Funny ha-ha or funny strange?" Bev asked.

"Funny. Humorous. Someone who can make a joke and take one."

Letting the door swing closed behind her, Carly followed Bev down the sidewalk toward Lakeford Park, a block from the office. Structured like a town square, the park was the primary destination for the nearby office workers looking for a comfortable place to enjoy the sun. A half dozen restaurants lined the shady square, most only open for lunch, though Lone Dog Coffee caught the morning rush, and Flippers—equipped with a liquor license—stayed open for happy hour.

Separating the tree-lined park from the soggy marshlands to the east was a paved jogging path that supposedly stretched all the way to the small airfield a few miles away, though Bev and Carly never cared to see for themselves. Between the plantar fasciitis that ailed Bev's feet and Carly's general hatred of exercise, the two always opted for the short route, which involved cutting off the jogging path at the far end of the park and circling through the square, picking up something for lunch on the way back around.

"I don't know." Bev shrugged. "I suppose I'd consider you funny."

"You *suppose?*" That didn't sound convincing.

"Yeah, I suppose. I mean, you wouldn't make my top-ten list of hilarious people, but you've had your moments."

Carly frowned as Bev picked up her pace, her blond pony-tail whipping like a pendulum once they crossed the street and started down the jogging path. Intent on losing the twenty pounds she'd gained since her wedding four years ago, Bev had more enthusiasm for their workouts, and Carly nearly had to break into a trot to keep up despite being five inches taller.

"Why are you asking me if you're funny?"

"Because Matt Jacobs thinks I'm not."

Bev eyed Carly inquisitively. "Since when do you care what he thinks?"

"I don't. I was just taken aback when he said he didn't think I was capable of making a joke."

The mere thought added pep to Carly's stride, irritation fueling an extra dose of adrenaline. Ever since Matt walked away from her cubicle this morning his comment had been stuck in her craw. "I can't believe he thinks that," she added.

"I can't believe it matters to you. You're fun, friendly, and everyone likes you. You don't have to be the office comedian, too. Besides, it's only his opinion."

"So you're saying he's wrong. I am funny."

Bev shrugged. "I'm saying, why the big fixation over Matt Jacobs and his opinion of you? Neil insults you all the time and you never bat an eyelash."

"Because Neil's always kidding. It's just his way."

And Neil wasn't the iron-chested, dark and studly sex magnate that ruled her dreams every night.

"Maybe Matt was kidding, too," offered Bev.

"He wasn't." Carly had played the conversation over in her mind a dozen times and remembered very specifically that he had not been kidding. He'd truly been shocked when she'd explained her joke about the survey.

And, of course, she also remembered the tiny flutters that had swept through her stomach when his shock transformed into pleasure. He'd almost seemed smitten with her, delighted to see a side of her he hadn't expected, and for a fraction of a second her body had responded with joy.

Until his words had sunk in and quickly squashed the moment.

"Forget what Matt said, I've got something bigger to talk about." Bev panted, her breath growing heavy as they followed the path along the edge of the marsh.

It had felt like a perfect spring day when they'd stepped out of the office, but now, in the high-noon sun, it was beginning to get warm. Carly noted with relief that they were only a short distance from where the path met up with the trees and the rest of their walk would be shaded.

"You've got scoops?" she asked.

"That compatibility survey they're making us do for the Singles Inc. project."

That got Carly's attention. Could they have picked the winners already? She'd thought they had through the week to complete the surveys.

"Remember Patty, my friend at Singles Inc.?" Bev huffed.

"Yeah."

"According to her, things aren't exactly as we were told." She glanced briefly behind them, then went on. "She heard one of the candidates had already been picked by Hall. This whole business about filling out the compatibility surveys is only to find out who's going to be on the project with him."

"Him?"

Bev tipped her sunglasses and flashed a blue-eyed glance at Carly. "Yeah, he's got the man picked out. Which means all the other men on staff filling out the surveys are just wasting their time. Their surveys won't even be considered, only the women's."

Carly shook her head. "I don't get it."

"The whole thing is a ruse, Carly. Hall's not looking for the two most compatible designers on staff, he's looking for the woman who most closely matches the man he's chosen for the job."

As Bev's words sunk in, an angry pool formed in Carly's stomach. "Don't tell me who the man is."

Bev nodded.

"You're sure it's Matt?"

"Positive."

Steam filled Carly's veins until she recalled her confrontation with Matt that morning and her anger turned to dread. She'd been so cocky about him having to fill out the survey to get the job, had accused him of trying to cheat even. And all the time Hall had already lined him up for the project.

She slowed her pace and sighed. How long would she continue to make a fool of herself in front of that man? It was bad enough infatuation turned her into a babbling idiot whenever he was around. Now the one moment she'd held her wits long enough to tell him off, she'd ended up being wrong about the whole thing.

It was too humiliating to consider.

"Does he know?"

"I don't think so. Patty told me they were keeping it really close to the cuff. Only she, her boss and one analyst there are aware of Hall's instructions on how to tally the surveys. In fact, now that I've told you, I've been ordered to kill you."

Carly would have laughed if she wasn't so dumbfounded, not certain whether she should wallow in embarrassment over popping off to Matt when she was the one with egg on her face or ire that once again he was being handed the big job.

Ire was winning by a nose.

"So all the surveys are for nothing?"

"All the men's surveys. The women's are legitimately being used to match against Matt's."

"I can't believe it," Carly fumed. She placed her hands on her hips and slowed down to a stroll. "Matt's walking away with another top project again."

"Matt and whoever strikes the closest match to his survey."

She stared out over the grassy lawn. The warm day had brought a crowd out from under the fluorescent canopies to enjoy lunch at the tables or hold an outdoor meeting. It was the first sign of spring, normally Carly's favorite time of year, but today even the good weather wasn't enough to hold up her spirit.

"Why do they think he's so great?" she asked. "So he's got, like, double master's degrees. Big deal. He's arrogant and flippant and not the least bit interested in sharing that wealth of talent with anyone else on the team. Why they keep raising the man to the level of he-god, I'll never know."

"He-god?"

Carly frowned. "You know what I mean. He doesn't deserve the constant accolades. There's a lot more to being a company asset than good Web design."

"True," Bev agreed, stepping over to a park bench and plopping down for a rest. "Though he's got a few assets someone's company would enjoy." She smiled as Carly sat down next to her. "You ever noticed him on casual Fridays? Man, does he have a butt for a pair of jeans."

Noticed? Carly had studied that butt so many times she could pick it out of a lineup. But this wasn't where she wanted the conversation to go. Matt Jacobs had had enough of her attention over the last two years. If there was ever a day to squelch it, today would be it.

"He used to play pro baseball, you know," Bev added. "Can you imagine that ass in a pair of those tight-knit baseball pants?"

The Anaheim Nationals, two years in their AA league before he'd been "cut loose," as Adam had put it. He hadn't said much more than that, just enough to feed a few steamy images of Matt in a uniform—and then out of it.

She shook off the thought, annoyed that she could be so easily pulled off track. This conversation wasn't about Matt's assets but how he'd become her personal liability. If this latest move by Mr. Hall wasn't enough to permanently exorcise her lust for that man, she seriously needed to consider psychotherapy.

"Can we get back to the subject, please? We're talking about Singles Inc. and who deserves that job. Mr. Hall lied to all of us. This project was supposed to be a fair game."

Bev blew out a sympathetic sigh. "I know, but in retrospect, none of this surprises me. It's our biggest account. There's no way Hall was going to let the project randomly go to two people on the staff. He needed one person in there as his anchor to make sure the job ran smoothly."

"And that anchor couldn't have been me?"

"Carly, they love your work. You and Matt are the two top designers on staff. They still consider you one of the best."

"They did before Matt came along. Now who knows what they think? I haven't had a challenging project in over a year. It's just the same old stuff, info screens without any user interactivity. How am I supposed to keep up my programming skills if I'm just putting graphics and text on pages?"

This job was not working out as she'd planned. She wasn't supposed to have hit a glass ceiling at the age of twenty-six. She was supposed to be on her way up the ladder, making the steady climb to bigger jobs and a bigger salary. Granted, she hadn't expected to spend her life working for Hall, but she'd thought as new opportunities opened up she'd continue to be in the running. But since Matt had come on board, her career seemed to have come to a screeching halt, and if she wanted to keep progressing, maybe it was time to accept the fact that she'd have to do it somewhere else.

"I'm tempted to quit."

Bev scoffed. "And go where? The high-tech industry is

barely picking up around here. To find anyone hiring, you practically have to move to Texas."

"I could go to Web Tactics."

"Rumor has it they aren't doing so well."

Carly'd heard that, too. Oh, who was she kidding? She'd just bought a house with a hefty mortgage. She couldn't risk losing it by leaving a secure job for something unknown. Wherever she went, she'd be the new gal on the team, the first one on the chopping block if a company decided to downsize, and with so many firms being swallowed up by the big fish or relocating out of state, she wasn't certain she could take the chance.

"I could move to Texas, but Mom and Jodi need me."

"They rely on you for a lot."

Carly sighed. She knew if she left Hall Technologies, she'd find a way to make things work, but making a move like that out of anger wasn't the smartest thing to do.

Right now she felt stuck, and if there was anything Carly hated, it was feeling trapped without choices.

"It's not fair," she said, the tone coming off whinier than she'd intended. "They should be giving everyone opportunities to be challenged. When they announced how they were handling the assignment of Singles Inc., I thought they'd finally seen that and done something about it." Gazing out toward a clump of cattails, she added, "I guess I was wrong."

"I don't know about that. I heard another rumor today."

"There's more?"

Bev nodded.

"Is it good news?"

"I don't know. It's all in how you choose to speculate."

Carly clasped her fingers around the seat of the wooden bench and braced herself. "What is it?"

"I heard Hall's planning to open a new management position."

"A manager?"

This *was* news. Mr. Hall had always preached the hazards of being top-heavy, which was why so far he only had two managers under him—Hugh Simonds, in charge of the programmers, and Frank Meyer, Carly's own manager and head of the creative-design team. The sales staff reported directly to Mr. Hall, as did Renee and Andrea, the two women who handled Human Resources and Payroll. The idea of a new position opening up was a big deal.

"Any idea who's getting the job?"

Bev shook her head. "Not a clue. I don't even know if he's planning to hire from within or bring in someone from the outside. But what I've heard is he wants to put together a team that exclusively handles the bigger projects and that he plans to assign the team a leader."

"A special project team, huh?"

"To take on jobs like Singles Inc. I guess he wants to keep moving in that direction."

The mention of Singles Inc. darkened Carly's mood. "And if he's thinking about hiring from within, you know what golden child he's got in mind."

Bev quickly held up a hand. "No one's said Matt's getting that job."

"But it's obvious he'd be considered. They're handing him Singles Inc., aren't they?"

Bev shrugged and Carly's infuriation mounted. "I'll kill myself if they give him that job."

"Carly, you're getting too far ahead of yourself. No one even knows if Hall's going to promote anyone on the team. He could have a golfing buddy or some IBM crony in mind.

Who knows? And if he was planning to promote from within, who's to say you wouldn't be considered? You've been here from the start, have handled just as many big projects as Matt has and you're a way better people person. There's a lot more to managing staff than technical expertise."

Carly knew that, but did Mr. Hall? And what if he did think technical skills mattered most? If that was the case, whoever handled Singles Inc. would have the best shot at proving themselves where that was concerned.

And she wanted a shot at that job.

She deserved it. In fact, she shouldn't even have to fight for it after all these years. She should simply get it. But apparently Mr. Hall didn't see it that way. Which meant she'd have to show him.

"I need to get on that project," she said.

"Huh?"

"Singles Inc. I need that job."

"Then you'll have to match Matt's answers closer than anyone else on the team."

Carly's hopes faded. "And of all the women on the team, I probably know the least about him."

"But you and I are the only women on the team who know he's the guy to match."

True, she did have that advantage. But unfortunately, thanks to a two-year-long resentment, coupled with her relentless attraction toward the man, she'd all but avoided Matt from the start. What she knew about him could be jotted down on a two-inch sticky note. She knew he was single, lived in an upscale condo down in Sausalito, drove a shiny BMW, had once played baseball and looked delicious in faded Levi's. That was the sum of her Matt Jacobs knowledge. Five basic facts. Plenty to feed her sexual daydreams but hardly enough to strike gold on a compatibility survey.

Attempting to change her answers to match his would be a total shot in the dark. Unless she had help.

"How close a friend are you to Patty?"

Bev shook her head in protest. "Oh, no. You could get in big trouble. Our company's image would be at stake, and you know how Hall feels about that. If Singles Inc. found out we'd tampered with their survey and it got back to Hall, heads would roll." She added with conviction, "I need my job and so does Patty. I can't ask her to get Matt's answers for you."

Carly frowned. "I won't ask you to, but it's so unfair. You know as well as I do, I deserve a shot at this. I was the lead Web designer before Matt stepped in, and you were just as angry as me when he kicked me off that first project by telling Frank he could handle it alone. We were supposed to work together on that."

"Jay-Lee Personnel Services. I remember that."

"I don't want you to do anything that would put your job at risk. Just help me brainstorm how I can swing this." Pushing off the bench, the two women returned to their workout, but this time headed back toward the office. "We still have through Thursday to finish our surveys, right?"

"I don't think that's changed. Holly and Paul are only coming back from vacation tomorrow. Hall wanted everyone to have an equal shot at the project."

Carly snorted. "Except for Matt."

What a joke, she thought, Mr. Hall making such a big deal out of the survey, how Singles Inc. had liked his idea so much they were considering developing a new survey designed for corporate teams. It was a huge publicity stunt, and in the end it was all a sham.

"Brian could get you in," Bev said.

Carly eyed her friend and grinned. Of course. Brian Shanahan, one of their programmers barely out of college, who prided himself for his hacking skills. And he was pretty good, too. Heck, knowing Brian, he'd probably already hacked into the database just to see everyone's answers.

"I don't know if I trust him to keep his mouth shut, though," Bev warned.

Good point, but Carly remained unfazed. "I'll take my chances."

"Really, Carly, you need to think twice about this. You could get in serious trouble."

"If I have to sit back and watch Matt walk away with both this project and a promotion, I'm not sure I want this job anyway."

"You say that now because you're angry, but think about your house and your family. Is it really worth the risk?"

One side of Carly would say no, but the other side wasn't about to get stomped on out of fear. Security was one thing, getting passed over for jobs she deserved called for taking a stand, no matter how she had to do it.

"I can't let this happen without putting up a fair fight. If Mr. Hall had Matt in mind for the project, he should have just assigned Matt a partner instead of dreaming up this stupid survey idea. And if I could say so to Mr. Hall without jeopardizing you, I'd do it."

Bev gasped. "Oh, you can't tell Hall what you know. He'd trail it right back to Patty in a heartbeat."

"Of course I won't. But that means I've got to even the

stakes my own way, because if I don't, if I keep sitting around letting them choose Matt over me, I'll never get anywhere in this company. And if I'm in a dead-end job, then I'm not risking much, am I?"

"I just worry what they'd do if they knew you tampered with the results. They went to great lengths to make sure everyone answered honestly. Remember that speech Hall gave about people comparing answers?"

Carly remembered it, though it seemed pretty hypocritical given what she knew now. Taking a deep breath, she elbowed her friend affectionately, Bev's warnings heeded but her decision made. "Then I'll just have to make sure I don't get caught."

3

CARLY OPENED THE door to a ringing phone. Hoping to catch it, she dropped her purse and take-out dinner on her entryway table, rushed to the kitchen and grabbed the cordless from the counter.

She'd had a private conversation with Brian Shanahan this afternoon, and he was all but certain he could get her the survey answers she wanted. If this was him calling already, he was better than she thought.

"Hello?"

"Hi, honey, it's Mom."

She dropped her shoulders. "Hey, Mom, what's up?"

"I just got Jodi's softball camp information in the mail."

"That's great. So we got her signed up in time."

As a sixth-grade-graduation gift, Carly had paid for her younger sister to attend a weeklong softball camp. It was, in a way, a gift to both Jodi and their mother, Jodi having dreamed of going all year, and their mother needing a break between working full-time, taking night courses at the JC and raising a daughter alone. As she'd had to scrape together the cost, Carly had just made the payment under the wire, so it was a relief to get the printed confirmation of Jodi's enrollment.

"Yeah, and she's thrilled. She's making you a special thank-you present for when you come over Friday."

Carly smiled. "That's sweet."

"But I was wondering if you could do me one more favor." Her mother sighed. "The strap on Jodi's backpack broke and there's no way to fix it."

"Does she need a new pack?"

"I remembered you'd said you were going to the outlet mall. Could you look for a purple backpack? I checked Deal-Mart but they didn't have purple, and I don't have the time to run around town looking for one."

"Sure, I can look around," Carly said.

"Would you do that for me? There's no rush. She can do with her old one for a while, but I've got finals—"

"Mom, it's no problem. I'll find Jodi a purple backpack."

"You're my saving grace, sweetheart. Listen, I've got to get dinner going before her practice, but we'll see you for Jodi's game Friday, right?"

"I'll be there."

"Love you, hon," her mother said before the phone went dead.

Carly pressed the off button, then placed the phone on its cradle and sighed. A purple backpack at the end of the school season. No problem.

Moving back to the entryway to fetch her dinner, she now wished she'd skipped the burrito and made something at home. She could use her seven dollars back. Not that she didn't make a good living at Hall Technologies. It was just that she had steep goals for her finances.

Carly insisted ten percent of her income went into a retirement fund. Add to that the two-bedroom bungalow she'd purchased last year, payments on her student loans, an unexpected transmission overhaul on her 2001 Grand Prix, and it was no wonder at the end of each pay period she was down to her last dollar. It didn't help that her mother and sister were barely scraping by thanks to a father who considered child support optional.

It was a constant struggle for Carly, trying to help her family on one hand yet still protect herself from ending up like her mother—unskilled, unsupported and still in love with a man who'd never learned to care for anyone but himself.

Not as hungry as she'd been a moment ago, she picked up the paper sack and carried it into her pale pink kitchen. If things kept going the way they were, she'd have to live with the previous owner's decor longer than she'd hoped—a fact that could likely cause her to go insane.

Though the house had come with a good-size yard and solid bones, cosmetically it was like living inside a giant bottle of Pepto Bismol. To say the former owners liked pink was an understatement. Every room had been painted, floored and tiled in some various shade of fuchsia, and though Carly had made progress in some rooms, ripping up carpet and priming walls, the kitchen and lone bathroom still thrived in their pristine bubblegum state. Only one corner of her eat-in kitchen had seen the threat of demolition, and that was where Bev had tried to tear off a loose corner of wallpaper, only to discover that beyond that four-inch square, the cheery pink teapots with the pale violet flowers were virtually cemented to the drywall, destined to rival the ancient pyramids in their time-tested strength.

But that was okay. Carly owned the home, and that was all that mattered. She'd qualified for the mortgage with her salary alone and, in the process, bought a slice of land in an old but desirable Marin County neighborhood. It was the security she'd never had growing up, and once she doubled the value with her pink-extinguishing transformation, it would be the bank account she'd never had, as well.

She unrolled the burrito from the foil paper and plopped it on a plate. The rustling in the kitchen was like a dinner bell for her cat, Mr. Doodles, who didn't waste time jumping up on the counter to see what she'd prepared.

Carly pushed the cat to the floor and spat, "Bad kitty!" but her efforts to train the cat had long become futile. Mr. Doodles— the name given the gray tabby by her little sister Jodi—was a horribly ill-behaved cat who roamed the house as if he owned it and did as he pleased. Carly had no idea how to correct his behavior, none of the advice she'd been given making any lasting progress. So she'd begun to accept the fact that Mr. Doodles wouldn't change and she'd have to love him despite his faults.

Moving to the fridge to fetch him his own dinner, her phone rang again, and Carly assumed her mother had forgotten to mention something else.

"Hello?" she asked, crinkling the foil in one hand and dropping it in the wastebasket.

"I'm in."

She paused for a moment, not immediately recognizing the voice.

"Brian?"

"I amaze even myself sometimes."

Yes! she thought. She hadn't wanted to get her hopes up even though Brian had assured her he could get to the Singles Inc. database where they'd input their answers. With his frat-boy immaturity, she sometimes suspected Brian overstated his abilities.

"You've got Matt's answers to the survey?"

"I've got everyone's answers to the survey. They've used a special code to isolate ours from the main population."

Her excitement was tempered by a flush of heat to her cheeks. It hadn't occurred to her that by asking Brian to get Matt's survey answers he'd end up privy to all of them—including hers.

Oh, to heck with it. If Brian wanted a thrill over her answers, he could have it. Getting on this project was worth whatever he might end up thinking about her and her sexual outlook.

"There's just one problem."

"Problem?"

"Do you have Matt's code name?"

"Code name?"

"Remember the code names Hall gave us to protect our privacy? That's the only identifying information attached to each person's survey. I couldn't decipher individual workstation IDs—which is actually impressive. Singles Inc. has some pretty decent security considering they designed this in-house. I don't usually see homegrown applications this good."

"So what does that mean?"

"It means unless you know what code name Matt was given, we can only guess which one is his."

Carly's mind raced in search of a solution. There had to be a way to figure out which survey was Matt's.

"How many people have filled out the survey so far?"

"Sixteen, which is two short of the people we have on staff. I'm guessing that's Holly and Paul."

The number didn't surprise her. She'd asked around this afternoon, and though the survey had been optional, everyone had decided to fill it out, curious to be included in the results. Even though a few weren't terribly interested in the project, everyone wanted to know who they most closely matched at Hall Technologies, if just for the fun of it.

"Now, we could eliminate some through logic," Brian added. "I know mine, you know yours, and I can obviously separate the men and women based on the code names." Since Carly was given the code name *Gidget,* she guessed Brian was right. "But that's still leaving you with almost ten men. You'll have to find a way to get his name without raising suspicion."

She stared at her pink linoleum floor, disappointed but not defeated. Though she had no idea how, sometime between now and Thursday she'd get Matt's code name. Already several ideas spun through her brain—all of them bad, but ideas nonetheless. She'd simply have to give it more thought, maybe consult with a trusted friend or two, but some way she'd figure it out. This was her career, her financial stability and her future at stake, all three of those things definitely worth it.

Two days to get one silly little code? No problem.

MATT LOOKED UP from his computer screen to see a pair of beautiful aqua-blue eyes staring back at him over the cubicle wall.

The sight gave him a start. Carly Abrams had never paid him a visit, nor had those dark coral lips ever been curved in a smile while pointed in his direction. Which meant he'd either fallen asleep at his desk and was dreaming or something strange was up.

She circled around and stepped into his cube, giving him a close-up view of his very favorite shirt—a low-slung wraparound that hugged her curves and accentuated her breasts in a way that should be outlawed in the workplace. The whole thing was held together by a simple bow at the waist, a bow that taunted him with the knowledge that just one tug could expose the delightful presents inside.

He dragged his eyes away and looked up at her smile. "Carly," he said, the word raspy from a mouth that had just gone dry. He cleared his throat and straightened in his chair. "What can I do for you?"

"I was wondering if you were through with my book. I need to take a look at it."

"I put it back on your shelf yesterday."

Her brows arched and those soft lips formed an O, the way they did in the fantasy he hadn't been able to shake since he'd seen those two blasted survey answers yesterday. Except, in his dream it was the look she had after he drizzled caramel syrup on her breasts and topped his Carly sundae with a dollop of whipped cream.

"Stupid me, I didn't even look." She shrugged her shoulders and chuckled nervously. "I get distracted and lose half my brain."

He knew the feeling. It was the same thing he'd been dealing with since it had sunk in that his available and most desirable coworker had a secret fetish for kinky sex. It had culminated this morning around two o'clock, when he'd been startled out of a dead sleep by a hard-on and the echoing sound of Carly Abrams's orgasmic screams.

And he'd been walking bull-legged ever since.

It was difficult enough trying to focus on the job this morning; that she'd picked today of all days to make her maiden voyage to his side of the floor had to be some sort of cosmic joke.

She leaned against his desktop and casually crossed her long, slender legs. Her silky flowered skirt reminded him of a cottage garden, and he tried hard to restore the longtime image he'd had of her. The safe image. The one that allowed him to forget the sexy body and concentrate on getting ahead at the firm. Mary Quite Contrary, the sunny, friendly girl-next-door who always referred to Brayton as Mr. Hall, brought in plates of homemade zucchini bread and gave people rides to the mechanics when their cars were in the shop.

"Well, um, since I'm here…" she said. "About yesterday—I was out of line and I wanted to apologize."

He blinked. "Yesterday?"

"You know, about the survey, you having to compete to get the Singles Inc. job." She fidgeted with the edge of his desk, trailing a finger along the grain of the fake oak veneer. "You caught me at a bad time. I was cranky and it was rude of me to take it out on you. So I just wanted to say I'm sorry."

Matt tried hard to rewind the whole incident. Yes, she'd popped off in a way that had had him questioning her stability, but he knew he'd been the one to start it by teasing her about her survey answers. If anyone should apologize, it should be him.

"I hadn't exactly started the conversation off on the right foot," he admitted.

"But that was no excuse for attacking you like that, so…" She let go of the desk and held out a hand. "Truce?"

He stared at those slim fingers, those perfectly polished nails, and found it ironic that she'd come here seeking exactly what he'd hoped to accomplish yesterday. His attempt at broaching a friendship had failed, but if things went his way, she'd be his employee very soon, and he should thank the stars for this second chance.

Taking her soft hand in his, he gave it a welcome shake, trying hard to ignore his body's reaction to the sizzling warmth of her touch. "Forgive me and I'll forgive you."

"It's a deal."

She slid her palm off his and smiled brightly. "So did you choose to fill out the survey?"

Straightening in his seat, he cleared his throat and said, "Yeah. I figured, why not?"

"So that makes everyone, then. I'm surprised. Some people don't like working on the bigger projects, but I guess it was the intrigue of the survey that had them going along."

"Hall did say something about everyone getting some sort of results."

"I heard that, too." She tucked a strand of brown hair behind her ear and nodded while she spoke. "I don't know what, though."

"Me, either," he replied.

Then an awkward silence fell between them. She glanced around his cube, trying to appear casual but not pulling it off, and the longer she stood there tapping a fingernail on his desktop, the more Matt began to wonder what she was really doing there.

He opened his mouth to inquire, but she cut him off.

"It sounds like Mr. Hall has an interest in movies."

He pursed his brow. "I didn't know that."

"Well, those code names we all got for the survey seem to be characters from films. At least that's what we're guessing." Grinning, she added, "Mine was Gidget."

Matt couldn't hold back his burst of laughter, though it occurred to him too late it might destroy their newfound truce—and the quirky look in her eyes said it might have.

"I'm sorry," he quickly shot out. "It's just so…perfect."

She shrugged good-naturedly, making Matt feel like a cad.

"I can't argue with that. I suppose some people might see me as…"

"Bubbly?" he offered.

A faint blush colored her cheeks, and he wished like hell he could learn to keep his mouth closed. For some reason, whenever she was near, he ended up either tongue-tied or blurting the wrong thing. It was the main reason he'd gone into Frank's office and asked to handle that first project on his own. He'd wanted to make a good impression at the new firm and he'd quickly discovered that wasn't going to happen in proximity to Carly, where his cock forever vied for attention and his brain wouldn't shift into gear.

Apparently, two years later, nothing had changed.

"Anyway," she said, "we've been comparing code names around the office. Do you know what Neil got?"

Matt shook his head.

"Patton!" She laughed more heartily than the situation warranted. "Is that a riot?"

"Yes, that's a good one."

"And who else?" she pondered, holding her chin and staring wistfully off into space. "Oh, Bev got Scarlett, and Brian got Hal. We're guessing Hal's the computer from *2001: A Space Odyssey*."

Matt nodded and smiled, trying to will himself to stay relaxed, keep his mouth shut and not inadvertently embarrass her again. If she agreed to work for him, he'd have to get past this magnetic field between them that continually garbled his thoughts and had him chewing shoe leather. But it wasn't easy when those breasts jiggled as she laughed or that flowery scent swarmed his nose, or those Caribbean eyes sparkled with such sweetness he wanted to scoop her up and take a bite or—oh, hell. Maybe they *were* better off hating each other.

Her smile slowly faded and she returned to the awkward fidgeting that had left him suspect before. Okay, so apology for yesterday accepted and a truce agreed. What was with the sudden small talk and this apparent desire to gab after two years of total avoidance?

"So what Hollywood feature did Mr. Hall put *you* in?"

He shook off his thoughts. "Pardon?"

"Your code name. Who did he give you?" Then she quickly held up a hand. "Not that you have to answer that. I realize they're confidential. We were just having fun with it, you know, seeing what Mr. Hall had assigned to each of us." Giggling, she added, "Heck, for all I know, his wife might have made them up. Or maybe he picked them off a list from Singles Inc." She blushed again and began to back toward the entrance to his cubicle. "Mr. Hall might not have picked them out at all. I don't think anyone asked. Or it could have been random or—"

"Rocky."

She stopped her rambling and stared. "Huh?"

"Rocky. He gave me Rocky."

Her mouth hung ajar for a moment before a twinkle lit in her eyes. It was a gleam too bright for simple amusement and it struck him as odd. Something was definitely hanging under the surface here, but what? She'd wanted his code name? It wouldn't get her anything without the password. So why the sudden interest in bringing him in on the office chatter?

"I like it," she said.

"Like what?"

"Rocky. I'd be flattered if I were you."

Matt hadn't given it any thought, though now that he did, he wasn't sure he agreed. "Rocky wasn't the brightest of bulbs."

She raised a sarcastic brow. "Neither was Gidget. But at least Rocky was a hero. He represented strength and determination."

Well, he might have that.

Taking a deep breath, she stepped back and clasped her hands into fists. "Well, I won't keep you any longer. I just wanted to apologize for yesterday and…"

"No problem."

She nodded. "Good. Well, I'll see you around."

Then she turned and walked—make that scurried—away. He watched her backside as she rushed quickly down the aisle before disappearing into the sea of cubicles, then he shook his head and settled back in his seat.

In his two years at Hall Technologies that was officially the strangest conversation he'd ever had, but at least it did one thing—it had momentarily taken his mind off the idea of her naked in his bed.

Now his thoughts were consumed with what exactly Carly Abrams was up to.

4

"THANKS FOR LETTING me use your computer." Carly tossed the comment over her shoulder to Bev, who was stretched out on the recliner in her den. "I really didn't want to do this at Mom's place with Jodi tagging at my heels."

When Carly bought her house and moved out of her mother's apartment, she didn't have the heart to take her computer with her. Jodi had grown attached to the games and her mom used it for schoolwork, and Carly knew if she took it, they'd go without, her mom barely affording the Internet service, much less the cost of a new machine. So Carly had insisted they keep it, reminding them she had a better machine at work and that she could come by and use hers whenever she needed to do something too personal for the office.

And changing her survey answers to coincide with Matt's definitely qualified as too personal for the office. It also qualified as too personal for her mother's apartment given that Carly knew the woman wouldn't approve of her little scheme.

Though Carly adored her mom, Carol Abrams was too idealistic for her own good. She thought hard work was all a woman needed to get ahead, that honesty was always the best policy and that good things came to those who waited.

Right. This from the woman who also thought that a cheating, irresponsible husband who waltzed in and out of his family's life would eventually come around once he'd sufficiently matured.

Carly's respect for her mother's ideals stopped about two clicks short of that one, and she'd also learned that sometimes to keep things fair a girl had to occasionally bend the rules.

"No, I don't think you want to explain some of those questions to Jodi," Bev said. "But I'm dying to see them myself. Did he fill out the whole survey?"

Carly unfolded the sheet of numbered answers Brian had given her and scanned the list. "He filled out everything."

"Then hurry and get to the good stuff. I can't wait to see what our hunky coworker has to say about sex."

Carly frowned and turned to Bev. "Don't forget you're married."

Folding her hands at her chest, Bev shrugged. "So. That doesn't mean I'm not curious. You've got to admit the guy's a hottie. Haven't you ever wondered what he might be like between the sheets?"

Carly's ears heated, and before she gave her secret away, she quickly turned back to the PC—a second too late.

"You have!" Bev gushed.

"I have not," Carly denied in a tone so unbelievable even she hadn't bought it.

"Yeah, right." Bev pushed out of the recliner and stepped over to the plate of cookies Carly had brought as thanks for the use of the machine. Picking one up, Bev eyed both sides of the chocolate-studded cookie.

"There's no nuts," Carly said.

"I was supposed to start a diet today, you know."

"It's Wednesday. No one starts a diet on a Wednesday."

"Mondays weren't working for me. I thought I'd give midweek a shot."

"Then put the cookie down and I'll take them home." Eyeing her friend sincerely, she added, "Really. I'm sorry. I thought your plan was to start with exercise this week, then diet next week."

Bev took a bite of the cookie, grabbed two more, then moved back to the recliner. "It is now. Besides, I need sugar to go with this new revelation about you and Matt."

"There's no revelation."

"You don't turn red as a cherry over a guy you're not interested in. I obviously hit a nerve." She flicked her brows. "I'm only wondering how deep it goes."

"Skin-deep," Carly affirmed. "I think he's attractive, that's it. And what woman wouldn't? The man's beautiful, but he's also a jerk, which makes him fun to look at and nothing more."

"He's not that bad, just a little driven. He might not mingle at the office much, but Adam says he's a great guy once you get to know him."

"Well," Carly said, picking up a cookie of her own, "I can get to know him pretty well right now."

She clicked into the Singles Inc. Web site and logged on to her profile. The sheet Brian had given her contained only letters and numbers for the answers, but Carly was able to translate them with ease by comparing her own survey results to the questions on the screen. It was a simple matrix of one through five, one being *Strongly Disagree* and five being *Strongly Agree*. True and false answers were coded using one for true and zero for false, and multiple-choice answers were recorded A through D. The Hall Technologies employees had been instructed to leave the narrative section blank, as well as the demographic data on marital history, race, income and other personal information not appropriate for this exercise. It was all straightforward. All she had to do was determine how closely she should match Matt's answers without going overboard.

"Start with the section on sex. How kinky is lover boy?"

Carly did as Bev suggested, curious herself. Would he be wild and naughty or was he a traditional kind of lover? Was he wine and roses or sun and fun? It hadn't occurred to her that she might not want the answer until she looked at the first question and the moisture drained from her mouth.

I tend to be conservative when it comes to sex.

He'd strongly disagreed, taking about a half dozen of her fantasies and throwing them into a big puddle of reality.

She double-checked the numbers, making sure she'd read them right, hoping she'd mixed them up. She didn't want Matt Jacobs to be the exact kind of lover she'd been looking for. If this worked out and she landed the project, she'd have to work with this man, speak coherently around him, possibly put in late hours…just the two of them…alone….

"Well?" Bev urged. "What does it say?"

Carly gulped. "That tall, dark and hunky has a wild side." And when she read his response to the next question, the temperature in the room crept up. "He's apparently open to all things kinky, too."

Bev let out an evil chuckle while Carly squirmed in her seat, the cookie in her mouth drying into pasty crumbs. She tried to tell herself this didn't mean a thing, that maybe Matt had simply followed her lead when she'd mentioned toying with Mr. Hall, but the fire in her cheeks and the tingling between her thighs kept calling her bluff. No matter how she turned this over in her mind, the survey stated clearly the last thing she needed to know right now—that Matt Jacobs could very well be the kind of sex toy she'd been looking for.

The cookie in her mouth turned to mortar, and, no longer hungry for food, she placed the remainder back on the plate.

"Does that surprise you?" Bev asked. "What man isn't into kinky sex?"

Pretty much every man she'd dated. At least it seemed that way. None of them had even mastered the straightforward kind of sex; what they'd do with a vibrator and a jar of chocolate body paint was anybody's guess. Needless to say, she'd never suggested it.

As if to torture herself, she eyed the next question. *I don't mind giving control to a trusted partner. Being dominated can be just as fun as holding the reins.*

He'd strongly agreed, lending even more weight to her little daydream involving feathers, a leather bustier and a pair of fuzzy handcuffs.

Her pulse kicked up a notch. Images sped through her mind, most notably one of Matt tied up spread-eagle on her bed while she worked his stiff cock with her tongue, then finished him off with a reverse cowboy—

She choked on a chocolate chip and Bev laughed.

"This isn't funny," Carly attempted, her brain going numb from lack of oxygen. A trickle of sweat beaded between her breasts. Why was it so hot in here?

"I think it's hysterical. You should see yourself—you're red as a beet. And don't rip a hole in my chair. We just bought that a few months ago."

Carly looked down to see her hands clasped tightly to the corners of the vinyl seat cushion. No wonder her fingers ached. Releasing them, she rubbed her sweaty palms on her jeans and attempted to brush it all off. These were just answers to a few silly questions.

In fact, this could simply be Matt's ego talking, a typical man with all bark and no bite, wishful thinking by a guy no better in the sack than half the other men in Marin County. Just because he claimed to have a fetish for kinky sex didn't mean he knew how to do it.

But you know he does.

She tried to shut out the little voice, the one that reminded her she'd always had that feeling about Matt, that he knew his way around a woman's body. He hadn't starred in a few fantasies for nothing. It had always been there, under the surface, the way he carried himself, the way he spoke with easy confidence, that casual calm one only walked around with when he knew he could deliver whatever he was dishing out.

Matt Jacobs would be good in bed, the best she'd ever had. If she'd been clinging to any doubt, these survey answers obliterated that chance. And thanks to it, she'd never be able to look the man in the eye again without choking on her own saliva.

"What about that question on the ideal romantic evening?" Bev asked.

Carly didn't want to look, now feeling as though she should leave this section alone and concentrate on the rest of the survey. Something told her he'd probably answered enough of the sex questions identically to hers anyway. Plus, she doubted Singles Inc. would even utilize this portion of the survey in their results. Most of the employees had probably skipped the section entirely.

But that didn't stop her eyes from darting down to the question Bev was referring to, the multiple choice which asked how the person would spend their ideal romantic evening.

He'd picked answer C: take-out dinner, candles and a bubble bath for two.

The exact same answer as hers.

Oh, man, she was a goner.

She tried to answer Bev's question but couldn't quite move her lips, and luckily she didn't have to. Like a knight in shining armor, Bev's husband, Kurt, stepped into the doorway, shifting the mood in the room and giving Carly a badly needed change of focus.

"I thought that was your car in the driveway."

She smiled and hoped her red cheeks weren't as obvious as they felt. "Hi, Kurt!" she squeaked.

His eyes drifted toward his wife. "Cookies for dinner?" he asked, teasing.

Bev smiled wide and motioned to the plate at Carly's side. "Help yourself."

"No, thanks." He rubbed his stomach. "What's really for dinner? I'm starving."

Rolling her eyes, Bev pushed up from the chair and made her way toward the door. "Let's go see what we've got," she said.

And then Carly was alone. Not wanting to interrupt Bev's and Kurt's dinner, she opted to skip the rest of the section on sexual habits and preferences and concentrate on the other parts of the survey to get this done as quickly as possible. It shouldn't take long to go through the answers and sync them up closely enough. If she just focused and hurried through it, she could be out of there in a matter of minutes.

She went back to the top of the survey and began running through Matt's answers, and it wasn't long before she noted that, aside from their sexual compatibility, she and Matt Jacobs had absolutely nothing in common. Practically every one of her answers had to be shifted from one end of the spectrum to the other, and Carly realized if she hadn't acquired his answers, she'd never have come close to being the most compatible.

He'd all but confirmed every impression she'd had of him—his selfish arrogance, his disinterest in others, his insistence in coming first in every aspect of his life. Matt Jacobs clearly cared about one thing and one thing only: Matt Jacobs.

I like helping others. Disagree.

I care what people think of me. Strongly Disagree.

I consider myself more intelligent than most. Agree.

I am attractive. True.

I've made sacrifices for my loved ones. False.

It went on and on, question after question painting the picture of the narcissistic, self-serving jerk she always suspected Matt was, and though a small piece of her felt the tug of disappointment, in general the survey brought her a giant breath of relief. Where his answers to the sexual profile had her wondering how she could come near him without tearing off his clothes and doing him on his desktop, the personality profile shriveled up her attraction and left her stale.

In part because she'd seen this man before—the striking good looks, the charming smile, the sultry voice, countered by a complete and total disregard for anyone but himself.

Matt Jacobs seemed to be a carbon copy of her father, and if Carly had one central goal in life, it was to never, ever end up like her mother.

A flood of relief swept through Carly, easing the tension in her neck and leaving her ripe with a giddy sense of elation. She'd caught Matt's number well before she did something stupid like act on her attraction. She was officially empowered, this survey handing her the emotional tool she needed to focus on the job and forget this latent lust she'd had for the man, kinky sex drive or not. He was a wolf in sheep's clothing, and unlike her mother, she wasn't fooled by the disguise nor ignorant enough to believe he could change.

The right man for Carly would be sexy and rugged but also caring and dependable. He'd put his family first, place her needs on the table right next to his and accept a partnership that involved both give and take. And if there was anything this survey screamed loud and clear, it was that Matt Jacobs clearly wasn't that man.

Energized with a new sense of control, she went through the rest of the survey, relating her answers more closely to Matt's, not copying verbatim but putting them close enough to appear the perfect match. Although, wondering how any woman would fit into the life of a man like him was a challenge. Guessing that the logic behind the survey was not so much to find matching answers but people who seemingly fit together, she took a calculated risk and set up her answers accordingly.

She was nearly done when Bev stepped back in the room and plopped down on the recliner.

Carly saved her answers and turned to her friend, who now looked a little ruffled. "Are you okay?"

Bev huffed. "Yeah, things have just been a little stressful around here lately with Kurt's new job, but it's no big deal." Picking up the cookie she'd left on the side table, she took a bite and added, "Just wait until you marry Mr. Right. You'll see what wedded bliss is really like."

Carly appreciated the sentiment, but when she boiled it down, she often doubted she'd ever find out. Marriage wasn't exactly on the top of her list. And in reality, for her there probably wasn't a Mr. Right. Every man too thrilling scared her witless, which left her with a plethora of safe but dull consolation prizes.

She didn't have to be a psychoanalyst to know her upbringing had left her destined to a life of independence. But that didn't matter to her. She was making her own home, providing herself with the kind of steady security she could count on. She had everything she needed when it came to home and family, and if there was a man out there to share it, he'd have to be one in a million. She wouldn't settle for anything less.

Closing down the Internet connection, she took the sheet with Matt's answers and glanced at them one last time. One in a million, that was for sure. And thanks to the survey, she'd been able to confirm that the small group of men good enough for her most definitely didn't include Matt Jacobs.

5

"YOU TWO ARE perfect for each other!"

Matt sat at the conference table staring at a gushing Brayton Hall, thinking that if the Singles Inc. survey pegged him and Carly as a perfect match, the company was headed for bankruptcy. He was about as suited to Carly Abrams as he was to putting on a tutu and dancing *Swan Lake*.

Which meant someone in this room was pulling a fast one on someone in this room.

He glanced around the table of suspects, which included Brayton, Andy McGee—the Singles Inc. marketing officer—and Carly, who didn't look the least bit fazed by any of this.

Did she know something he didn't?

"Who knew we had the ideal couple sitting right here in our offices?" Brayton added.

Matt studied Brayton's goofy grin and realized that no matter how hard the man tried to come off as a suave and polished businessman, he'd never fully conceal the boyish nerd he'd grown up as. Even if Matt bought the idea that these survey results were legit, they surely didn't warrant this giddy reaction from the boss. Yet here were Hall and Andy, donning dopey smiles like two kids who'd just caught him and Carly making out in the backseat of his Beemer.

Passing a sheet of paper that appeared to contain his compatibility rankings, Andy chimed in. "A match this close, we might lose you two to a honeymoon sometime soon." He turned to Brayton and chuckled. "I don't know, maybe this wasn't such a good idea after all. We need this project to stay on schedule."

Matt's left eyebrow rose involuntarily. Were they kidding?

"You don't have to worry about that," Carly said. "We'll be taking this project very seriously. Hall Technologies is excited to name Singles Inc. as one of its clients, and our priority will be assuring you're a satisfied one."

Andy winked. "Though a sidebar story about Singles Inc. finding everlasting love is always welcome, too. We have a habit of finding romance wherever we go. We are the experts, you know."

Matt had to swallow down a laugh. The guy was marketing to the core, always looking for that double bonus where publicity could be made. He was probably already sizing up how Matt's and Carly's faces would look plastered on the sides of every transit bus in the county.

"It's hard to argue with an expert," she agreed. "But why don't we put the job first and see what follows after?"

Cool as a cucumber. If Carly was at all suspect of these results she wasn't showing it. But before he could ponder why, she tossed him an alluring glance that he caught with an unexpected blood rush to the loins.

Damn, she was beautiful when she wanted to be. And today, in front of the boss and their client, she'd upped the volume on her charm. Matt only saw her like this on occasion, usually during staff meetings when heads began to butt and someone needed to step in and play referee. She was good at that, a born diplomat. The type who brought sanity to all things insane—like the direction Brayton and Andy were trying to take this meeting in right now.

Glancing down at the page Andy had slid across the table, he noted his compatibility results with the other employees— and, sure enough, Carly was listed on top with an eighty-seven percent match ratio. The next nearest was Laine, another coworker he'd crossed paths with on a couple projects. He'd liked Laine, enjoyed talking with her, and even she only ranked in at fifty-four percent. To think Carly could outmatch Laine by thirty-three percent was ludicrous at best. He'd stake better odds on aliens landing in Graceland and resurrecting Elvis.

Not that Carly didn't have any redeemable qualities. Make no mistake—the woman had a number of assets entirely compatible with his desires, and he suspected when it came to all things physical, they'd fit together quite well. Sneaking a peek down the ruffled neckline of her pale blue pantsuit, he could think of a couple things that might slip nicely into the palms of his hands. And the fruity look of those glossy pink lips was definitely harmonious with his taste for all things sweet.

But none of that took away from the fact that professionally they'd rubbed each other like sandpaper since the day he'd been hired. And the fact that she wasn't sitting there as bewildered as he by this whole compatibility thing left him smelling something foul.

Opening a purple folder labeled *Singles Inc.,* she pulled out a stack of what looked like business specifications. "I only had a moment to look these over, but I can already see how we can make improvements to your current software. Some of it is outdated. Not only that, but the site loads slowly. I'm gathering most of the graphics have a higher resolution than necessary. Believe it or not, a good portion of the country still connects to the Internet through dial-up. We'll want something that works fast."

Matt frowned and looked down at the papers in front of her. "Where did you get those?"

"A copy was left with both of us."

"When?"

Looking a little too self-gratified, she replied, "I take it you haven't been back to your desk in a while."

No, he hadn't. Though he'd known they were making announcements this morning, he hadn't been terribly interested, opting instead to play around in the lab, testing some animation on various platforms. He hadn't even known he'd been awarded the Singles Inc. project until Hall had popped in and told him about this meeting after noticing that Matt hadn't accepted the electronic calendar invite.

Not waiting for an answer, Carly turned back to Andy. "I see you've done some customer surveys for feedback on your current site. It would be nice to bring some of your clients back to look at the new prototype. Is that a possibility?"

"I'm sure we can arrange that."

"If not, we can gather our own group, but it's always best to work with people who've actually used the site," she said, jotting down something illegible on one of the pages.

She continued flipping through the pages of the proposal. Her copy was already riddled with notes, and Matt began feeling unprepared and a little foolish for showing up without so much as a pen. As the three of them spoke about the project, he alternately tried to keep abreast of what was going on while studying the papers in front of her, looking for something he could use to interject some thoughts of his own.

How did she manage to run away with this project so

quickly? It wasn't as if he'd been gone all morning. He'd only stepped away from his desk for an hour—two, tops—and here she was talking as though she were the team lead on this project instead of an equal partner.

And the obvious impression in Brayton's and Andy's eyes left him irked. He didn't like being one-upped, and after his baseball career had ended he'd sworn he'd never be less than best again. Yet here was Carly only minutes into their new joint venture, already grabbing the baton and running ahead without him.

He recalled his conversation with Adam in the restaurant the other day, how the buzz in the office had her as a contender for the management job opening up, and an annoying curl of resentment tightened his jaw. Over his dead body. He'd worked way too hard getting to the top of Brayton's list to let Carly Abrams pop out in front of him at the last furlong.

"What do you think, Matt?" Brayton said, pulling him from his thoughts. "I know you haven't gone through the preliminaries yet, but any initial thoughts on the subject?"

He looked around the table, all three of them staring at him in anticipation of his answer, but he hadn't heard a word they'd said.

"Well, um…"

As he fumbled for a reply, he caught a glint in Carly's eyes. She was batting a thousand; he was sinking like a brick, and she not only knew it, she was enjoying every minute. But before he could embrace his irritation, she stepped in and unexpectedly threw him a life preserver.

"I don't think their transition to Oracle will impact what we're doing, but you might have more experience than I do."

"Uh…no. We can feed data to Oracle just fine." And when he looked to her to confirm he was on the right track, she faintly nodded and encouraged him to continue. "Any software we use can accommodate your downstream system."

Andy appeared to be pleased with his answer. "That and our new logo are the only new developments we've got since the preliminary specifications were drawn up." He stacked his papers and placed them in his leather-bound notepad, then tucked the pen in its holder before closing the file. "So unless either of you have questions, we'll let you two review the documents more thoroughly and go from there."

Brayton picked up his BlackBerry and clicked a couple buttons before gesturing to Matt and Carly. "Schedule a meeting with me late next week to discuss your initial ideas."

Carly made another illegible note and nodded, and Brayton turned to Andy. "We'll get back to you shortly after."

"Good enough," Andy said, rising from the table. "I look forward to working with you two." Then, snapping a finger in their direction, he added, "I've got high hopes for that other thing, too."

Carly smiled and graciously accepted a handshake, but Matt couldn't temper his annoyance. No computer program was going to assign him a lover, particularly a woman who'd be working for him before the year was out. And though Carly might be showing patience with this lunacy, he'd heard enough.

Forcing a smile on his face, he said his goodbyes and stepped out of the conference room, shaking his head and wondering how his morning managed to get blown to bits in the span of one hour. He'd come into the office feeling pretty good, all but forgetting about Singles Inc. and their survey. He hadn't expected to be chosen for the project and had mentally wished good luck to whatever couple they'd selected.

Now he was walking out of a meeting he'd just blown on a project he didn't especially want, newly paired with a woman who was supposedly ideal for him despite the fact that she'd spent two years loathing him.

If that didn't spin a guy's head, what would?

"Matt!" Carly called out behind him as she rushed to catch up with his quickened pace. He reluctantly slowed, his mood a little too sour for conversation right now, but what else could he do, break out in a run?

Instead he turned and caught a glimpse of the one other major problem with this whole scenario—that he'd be working in proximity with Carly Abrams over the next several months. And given her ability to turn his thoughts in circles, he really didn't need to be put to the test right now. He was trying to impress the boss, not look like an ass in front of him, and though he'd wanted to work with Carly someday, he'd prefer doing it *after* he landed the promotion.

A side of him thought he should just take her home to his condo, strip them both naked and not come out until he'd completely and thoroughly sweated her out of his system. But looking in those sultry blue eyes, the loose strands of satiny hair framing her face and that silky blue pantsuit hugging every curve, he doubted even that idea would prove fruitful. It would only make him want her more, which was why the coming months were most likely going to be hell.

He could see it play out before him clear as day, his history coming back to haunt him, his propensity for putting his wants ahead of his needs and ending up with nothing. Ever since he'd been released by the Nationals he'd promised himself he'd take his next career seriously. Never again would he be told he had the talent but not the discipline to make it.

It had been hard enough letting go of the one thing he was good at, and now that he'd found a new career he wasn't about to screw it up. This time he'd be the best. He'd scale to the top, look in the mirror and see a sense of pride staring back at him instead of the bloodshot dismay of a self-induced failure.

And the temptation standing in front of him had the power to derail it all. Because when he looked at Carly Abrams, the last thing he wanted to think about was work.

"What's your schedule look like?" she asked, using a delicate finger to shift the hair away from her face. "We'll need to get together before we meet with Brayton."

Those blue eyes were all business, and once again it struck him how casually she was taking the news of this survey. An eighty-seven percent compatibility rate wasn't typically brushed off when both people involved happened to be single and available.

Instead of answering her question, he leaned a hand against the wall and asked, "So what do you think about this survey? You think it's legit?"

She shrugged casually, though he noticed a faint blush coloring the tip of her nose. "They'd said in the staff meeting a lot of the questions had been ignored. They only pulled out pieces they felt were pertinent to the work environment."

"So they ignored the section on sex?"

The blush on her nose spread to her cheeks. "I can't see how that would apply to work."

"Which means our scores could have gone even higher."

She swallowed.

"Or lower."

He stared her down, a knowing look crackling between

them as he sank his gaze into those deep baby blues. He couldn't deny their sensual chemistry. It thickened the air and heated the space they encompassed, and unless he'd completely lost his touch with women, he'd bet she sensed it, too. The rise and fall of her chest had gone shallow, her breath growing faint as he stood inches from her breasts. She always seemed to tense up around him as if she were holding something back, and a side of him wanted to yank off the restraint and see what she held inside. Her eyes stayed fixed on his, speaking words he couldn't quite hear, whispering something sweet yet too softly to decipher.

Take away their bitter differences and there was definitely promise there. But as much as he'd like to explore that path, what he really needed to uncover was what she thought about this survey so they could clear the air and get down to the business of this project.

Was she being the good corporate soldier, going along without asking questions? Or was she skeptical, like him, and wondering what kind of fast one was being pulled on them both? Because, heat or no heat, buying a match that high was simply out of the question.

"That percentage is pretty high," he said. "Almost…unbelievably."

Her eyelids began to flutter. "Like I said, who knows how much of that survey they used. If they'd used all the answers, the results might have ended up very different."

"Yes," he agreed, still trying to read her expression but not knowing her well enough to trust his instincts fully. His gut told him he was getting a practiced line, but he couldn't put money on it.

"Hey, you two, get a room."

He glanced over his shoulder. It was Craig Hale winking and wearing a wide grin.

"Get a room?" he asked.

Instead of answering, Craig simply began humming the Singles Inc. television jingle as he slipped by and continued down the hall.

Carly didn't look amused. "That's right—you missed the meeting this morning." She sighed. "The survey results have made us the latest in watercooler humor. I'm hoping everyone loses interest over the weekend."

Still watching Craig disappear down the aisle, he said, "Sounds like I picked a good meeting to skip."

"Yes, and why did you, by the way? People have been itching all week for those survey results. I thought you would have been there, as well."

Matt shrugged. "I didn't figure I'd get the job."

Her eyes darkened and in an instant the mood cooled. "So you didn't go to the meeting because you didn't think it would be about you."

"No. Not exactly. I just…" He searched for a way to rephrase that but came up empty. Okay, maybe that was true. Maybe he hadn't been interested in Singles Inc. or who got the job because he'd expected it wouldn't be him. Too many other people in the office had been likelier choices. But he wouldn't have said it like that.

"I had better things to do." There. That was much better.

"Like what?"

"Like my job."

There was that glare again. What was this woman's problem with him? One moment he could swear the space around them was about to ignite, the next she was scoffing him off as a cad.

Opening her folder, she flipped to a page that looked like a print of her calendar. "I'm open early next week. Will that be enough time for you to look over the project documents?"

"Ample."

"Then how about I schedule some time for us to get together?"

"My schedule's open."

She forced a smile. "Okay, then. I'll do that." Then she stepped past him and strode back to her desk without another word.

Great. His first team project at the firm had already started off on two left feet, and they were barely an hour in. And they were supposed to be perfect for each other? If this was their idea for right, he'd hate to see wrong.

"WHERE ARE YOU?"

Carly pressed her cell phone to her ear. She could barely hear the caller over the screams of a nearby toddler clutching a pink-and-yellow soccer ball in her aisle of Thriftees Sporting Goods. Carly moved on to an area quiet enough to continue her conversation.

"Bev, is that you?"

"Where the heck are you, in a torture chamber?"

"The toy section at Thriftees, so I guess that would be a yes." Zigzagging down the aisles, she added, "Did you know there isn't a single purple backpack for sale in the entire San Francisco Bay area?"

"Did you try Deal-Mart?"

"I've tried everywhere, but I'm going back there right now. At least the one I saw there had a couple of pretty purple flowers on it." She all but ran toward the exit.

The double doors slid open and she stepped out into the heat of an unseasonably warm evening, enjoying the weather while it lasted. Anyday now the fog would return over Marin County, bringing a chill to the evenings again, but for now she was comfortable in shorts and a tank top even though it was nearly eight o'clock.

"What's that sound? Are you eating?" Carly asked.

"Uh-huh," Bev said. "I found a box of Froot Loops in the back of the pantry. I'm a little stressed out right now. They're talking about cutbacks at Kurt's work, and he's the new guy on the job." Carly pulled out her car keys and unlocked the door to her Grand Prix, sliding behind the wheel and starting up the engine as Bev continued. "Kurt says not to worry, but you know me."

"If Kurt says not to worry, don't. He'll be fine. He always lands on his feet."

"Yeah, and I always end up gaining fifteen pounds in the process." After another moment of crunching, Bev added, "But seriously, I wasn't calling about that. I wanted to know how your meeting went with Matt. I was surprised he didn't show for the meeting. Do you think he knew he'd already been chosen?"

"It didn't seem like it when we met this afternoon. I think he genuinely didn't expect to get the project, so he didn't give a squat about who did." Shaking her head, she muttered under her breath, "How self-absorbed is that?"

She backed out of the parking space and made her way through the lot.

"Do you think anyone suspects you tampered with the survey?"

"Not a bit. In fact, you should have seen Mr. Hall. He was crazy over the fact that Matt and I matched so closely. He and Andy McGee were practically giddy, which was a little weird."

"And what about Matt?"

"I think he was skeptical at first, but I put that to rest after the meeting." Carly smiled as she waited at the light. "You should have seen me. I was smooth as silk."

"You?"

Carly didn't miss the humor in the tone. "Yes, me. I can pull off a scam on occasion, and this was one of them. Basically, the project is mine and all worry and doubt are behind me."

"You sure? I was a bit concerned when I saw how high you two matched. You didn't have to come that close, you know."

Accelerating into the on-ramp of Highway 101, Carly relaxed and headed north for the purple-flowered backpack. "Trust me, this deal is signed, sealed and delivered. Hall has completely bought into this. As of this afternoon, how I got on the project is history. Now my only task will be dazzling the boss with my talents."

"So you did it. You actually pulled this off."

"Oh, yeah. I'd say it's safe to declare this round a victory."

6

MATT SPENT THE BETTER part of Monday going over the preliminary specifications for the Singles Inc. job. The next time he had a meeting with Brayton and Andy, he intended to have his bases covered, so he went over every page, making notes along the way. Then he read it all again before he felt satisfied he'd gotten the gist of what they were looking for and a solid outline of discussion points and ideas. And when he was done he leaned back in his chair, rubbed his face in his hands and decided he needed a break, which for him meant heading back to the lab.

He loved the lab, the large project room used primarily to store their servers and test programs on various platforms. It was a quiet place where he could get away from the chatter and lose himself in his work. Slightly cooler than the outside offices, the temperature kept him alert in the afternoon when his energy dipped, and the hum of the PCs and servers created a soothing white noise that helped him think.

Since most programmers on staff were familiar enough with how their site designs would translate to other operating systems and browsers, the lab wasn't used often, which meant Matt was often alone.

Long and rectangular, one end of the room held a coffee table, a couch and four stuffy chairs, old furniture from the

Lake Tahoe cabin Brayton's wife had remodeled. In the center was a large project table. The other side of the room was partitioned off to house the company servers, as well as shelves full of spare cords and boneyard equipment, broken, outdated and waiting for the annual recycling drive.

But Matt's favorite spot was at the helm of the dozen or so Macs and PCs that lined the long wall. Over the vinyl tile flooring he could roll from workstation to workstation, whisking his chair back and forth, doing three things at once like Mr. Spock at the console of the starship *Enterprise*. In this room he got in his groove, trying an animated graphic on one PC while dicing through a digital photograph on another. Only a dozen computers could keep up with him when he got on a roll, and it was then when he felt the rush he used to feel back at the plate, back in the days when he hadn't yet learned to appreciate the natural gifts he'd been given.

But Matt was luckier than most. When he'd blown his first career in baseball, he'd discovered another in photography and Web design, and being smarter than he'd been the first time around, he had no intention of taking this second chance for granted.

Taking his seat at the helm, he loaded Photoshop on one PC, then brought up Flash on another. He'd been working on a Web site for ErgoSystems, a local energy company in the East Bay, and given the new assignment on Singles Inc., he'd be turning this one over to Neil to complete. But before he did, he wanted to have the primary design in place. He'd just clicked to bring up the program from the server when he heard the door behind him and turned to see it was Adam.

"What brings you to this corner of the floor?" he asked.

"You, and a little information I thought you might be interested in."

Adam stepped over to the couch and took a seat, lifting a basket of stress toys Hall kept on the coffee table before tossing his feet up. Sifting through the basket, he bypassed a number of small handheld massagers and squishy balls and pulled out a Slinky.

"Information?"

Eyeing the partition at the other end of the room, Adam asked, "We alone?" When Matt nodded, he went on, "I got a line on the Singles Inc. survey that put you and Carly together."

That got Matt's attention.

"What about it?"

"It seems one young and cocky programmer by the name of Brian Shanahan was overheard leaking the fact that he'd hacked into their databases last week." Adam toyed with the Slinky in his hand, his expression practically smitten. "And, when pressed by yours truly, he told me everything he knew—confidentially, of course."

"Of course."

"When you suspected something fishy? You were right. Those survey results were the fine work of one Carly Abrams."

"I knew it!" Matt said, slapping a hand to the table. "I could have bet money that survey was rigged."

"Rigged by your new partner."

"You wouldn't kid me about this."

Adam sobered and held up two fingers. "I swear this is no joke. I wouldn't do that to you, pal."

Matt shook his head, not certain whether to be relieved, angry or bewildered by the news.

On one hand, he was thankful those survey results hadn't

been for real. He'd been distracted by that prospect all weekend. Life was hard enough at the office trying to keep his interest in Carly strictly business.

On the other hand, what kind of man could turn down the perfect woman? Particularly a man who had ideas of having a family someday. Granted, now wasn't the ideal time for him, but he knew that rarely did the right woman come along at exactly the right time. Usually it happened when a guy wasn't looking. He'd gone over that scenario a dozen times, recalling oft-told stories of friends who'd been hit by Cupid's arrow when they'd least expected. By Sunday afternoon Matt had nearly convinced himself Carly Abrams was the One and that he was starting off his week having to deal with the idea that his perfect mate might be standing in the way of his perfect career.

Now he didn't have to. His initial instincts had been right on target. Carly was a woman he could definitely create some heat with, but that's where their compatibility ended.

But that didn't explain the situation.

He looked inquisitively at Adam. "What exactly did she do? And why?"

Adam's smile widened. "Apparently, she discovered Hall had already picked you for the Singles Inc. project."

"Is that true?"

Adam scoffed. "Come on. Did you really think they'd put just anyone on the biggest account we've acquired to date?"

Matt guessed not, and as it all sank in, it began to make more sense. He had been Hall's number-one man since signing on with the firm, and these were the types of projects he'd been hired to take on.

"You were given that job before they even came up with

the survey idea, according to what Brian heard. And Carly wanted it, too." He slipped the Slinky back and forth between his hands. "She figured the only way to make sure she got the project was to cheat her way in."

Matt's eyes narrowed. "That's the same thing she'd accused me of trying to do last week."

"Ah, deflect the guilty by blaming the innocent. Clever."

"And she almost had me, too." Matt leaned back and propped his feet on a spare chair. "Are you sure this is all true?" he asked. "Where did you say you heard this?"

"Right from the horse's mouth...*Rocky.*"

"No way!"

"Though it is just Brian's word, I don't know why he'd lie about something like that."

Matt would have taken the opportunity to agree with his friend, but he was too distracted by this new information—most notably, what he should do about it. There was no way he'd see this project to completion letting Carly think she'd gotten one over on everyone. And he knew for a fact that's exactly what she thought. She'd been smooth as cream in the meeting with Andy and Hall, practically serenading them with her charm and wit.

Annoyance burned in his gut. If those two only knew what she'd done, they'd bounce her off the job quicker than one of his fastballs. And if he was the jerk she thought he was, he'd be the first in line to tell them.

But he wasn't.

He was better than that. But just because he had no intention of ratting her out didn't mean he'd let her get away with it. She'd screwed with him and this project, and a move like that deserved some sort of payback.

And Matt had just the thing in mind.

Carly Abrams wanted everyone to think the two of them were compatible. Then that's exactly what she'd get.

STOP BY THE LAB when you get a chance. Matt.

Carly held the sticky note she'd found on her computer as she walked down the long aisle toward the lab. Matt had all but disappeared recently, and she'd been on the cusp of worrying that this working relationship would fall flat before it got started. Matt wasn't considered much of a team player and he especially hadn't come across warm and cozy over the idea of working with her. The note at her desk had lifted her spirits and given her hope that even if she wasn't his first choice for a partner, he'd at least planned to work with her on this.

She pushed open the door to the lab, and he greeted her with a wide grin that tipped her off balance. For a short beat she felt compelled to stand and stare.

The sight was nearly awe-inspiring, those gunmetal-gray eyes tipped up at the corners and those sinful lips curved into a smile. She wondered how anyone could deny him when he beamed like that and she found it a shame he didn't show this side more often. A look that powerful got a man anything he wanted—but to her knowledge, he never put it to use around here.

Which was a good thing for her. When Matt was around, she already had a habit of forgetting her name; she didn't need a regular dose of this charm obliterating her senses completely.

"Come on over," he said. "I've got some samples for you to look at." He was sitting in front of a PC, and as she stepped toward him, he grabbed a chair and wheeled it up to his side. "I took the new Singles Inc. logo and have been testing it against different color schemes. I'm curious to know which one you think we should go with."

He began hitting keys on the PCs to bring up the sample Web pages so they could view them side by side, and while he tinkered with one, she took the seat he'd offered, using the motion to scoot slightly away. It was bad enough he looked so good, he smelled good, too, and if she intended to keep her mind on business, a little distance would be in order.

Unfortunately, Matt didn't share the same concern. After bringing up three screens to his left, he made his way toward her, leaning over to click into the Macintosh at her right. His thigh grazed her knee, the sensation of that simple touch splaying like sparks through her. She was about to scoot away farther, but he placed a casual hand on the back of her chair and reached over to the next PC, flashing one hard, molded chest squarely into view.

Her mouth watered. He'd unbuttoned his shirt just far enough to show off a dusting of chest hair, and she clasped white knuckles to the arms of her chair so her hands wouldn't act on the impulses shooting through her head. Bent over like this, it would take nothing to sink her fingers into that dark, shiny hair, grab a hand to his jaw and devour him in one needy gulp. And she was almost desperate enough for excitement to do it. Without a doubt, Matt Jacobs would be a thrill, the mere thought halting the breath in her lungs.

He had sculpted biceps, muscles twisting in hills and valleys down those hard, rugged arms. For a fleeting second she wondered how they'd feel wrapped around her naked body. Carly had a fantasy about being bound and taken by a warrior lover, and those arms filled every corner of it. She imagined them holding her firm, keeping her captive and forcing her to accept the delicious sensations until she grew mad with desire, her writhing body no match for the force of his will. He'd torture her with that sensual mouth, invade her with his thrusting cock and silence her screams of delight with his hot, probing tongue. And then, only when she was fully spent and utterly—

"So what do you think?"

She jumped. "Huh?"

He gave her a curious look. "Earth to Carly. Did I lose you to something more interesting than our Web site?"

Absolutely.

"Oh. No." She giggled like a preteen. "I was just thinking about something." Clearing her throat, she released her hands from the chair and adjusted in her seat, hoping the motion might ease the throbbing that had propped up between her thighs. "Let me see," she said, gradually returning to reality and the six computer screens in front of her.

She pointed to one. "I think the red one is very sexy." Then she pointed to another. "But that olive-green makes a nice contrast to the logo."

Matt returned his arm to the back of her chair. "My thoughts exactly." Then, giving her a wink, he added, "Maybe we really are as compatible as everyone thinks."

She blinked. "Who, me and you?"

"Yes, me and you."

There was a look in his eyes she didn't know what to do with, serious yet playful, maybe a bit sultry. She wasn't sure if it was real or her imagination cutting in thanks to his nearness, but it definitely seemed as if something was lurking in his gaze.

"Well, I told you that survey can't be counted on for much," she tried.

He rolled his chair a little closer.

"Funny thing about that. I've been talking to Terry Haynes—the programmer over at Singles Inc. I asked him for a small favor."

She held her breath. "A favor?"

"Yeah. I asked him to run our surveys using all our answers. You know, just to dispel all the chatter going around about you and me."

She gulped. "And?"

"And our percentage went up. Ninety-one percent when all was said and done."

Guilt lodged in her throat, causing her to choke out a cough. "That's hard to believe." She swallowed the hoarseness from her voice. "There must have been a mistake."

He inched closer until the arms of their chairs were touching. "I'm beginning to think the mistake is you and I ignoring the obvious."

She tried to nudge her chair away, but all the strength had drained from her legs. "Come again?"

Those gray eyes darkened, and the playfulness that had been there a moment ago turned into something smoky. With his chair as close as it could get, he bent in to narrow the gap between them, putting her nerves on red alert.

"You forget that I saw a couple of your answers to the survey." He dropped his eyes to her lips. "I don't think you were toying with Hall when you answered those questions on sex." Then he dropped them lower. "I think you were telling the truth."

She dug her fingers into her chair.

He inched closer.

"I think you and I might really be perfect for each other. Don't you?"

"It's only a silly survey," she squeaked.

One corner of his mouth cocked into a smile. "I don't think there's anything silly about this heat between us. I think we might do ourselves justice by seeing where it goes."

His brow arched and then twitched as he waited for her answer, but Carly was tongue-tied.

She really should object, knowing what she knew about the survey. A decent woman would. But as much as she tried to deny it, with Matt she didn't want to be decent. She wanted to be delightfully bad. Because no matter how wrong he was about the results, there was one thing she couldn't deny: she hadn't lied on all the questions.

When it came to the section on sex, she and Matt truly had been the perfect match.

Her pulse revved up a few RPMs, leaving her fighting for air in the little space between them. He'd closed in on her, placing that delectable body on dangerous ground. His lids grew heavy, his gaze trailing a heated path down her chin, over her shoulder and across her breasts. He seemed to be gathering ideas along the way, and an ache in her chest begged to know each and every one.

"What did you have in mind?" she asked, not recognizing the low voice that seemed to come from her throat.

That playful look came back to his eyes. "Maybe we should go lock the door, rip our clothes off and see exactly how compatible we really are."

"Are you kidding?"

That hadn't been a scoff so much as a confirmation. With his rugged scent drugging her thoughts, his breath tickling the edge of her neck and those muscled arms twitching with anticipation, she was seriously considering doing this.

And why not? It was only sex. Wild, kinky, in-the-office-during-business-hours sex. The kind she'd been dreaming about since she'd realized she had a sex drive. For ages she'd been waiting for something exciting to happen to her, and now that it had, she'd forever kick herself if she dared turn it down.

His fingers touched her chin and she nearly collapsed from the jolt that ran through her. He'd tipped his head toward her and now his lips were on the verge of touching hers, whetting her appetite for the smorgasbord of pleasure she knew this man could offer.

So what if the survey was a sham? The speeding thrill whipping through her was entirely real. After years of yawn-inducing sex, she had a real man at her fingertips. A dark, fiery man. The kind that scorched the air around her, soaked her wet with just a look and set her body ablaze.

This was the breathless life she'd been waiting for, and all she had to do was pucker up and take it.

Cupping her cheek, he brushed his thumb over her lips, and when he acknowledged that he hadn't been kidding, she opened her mouth and drew it inside, stroking her tongue against his flesh to mirror what she'd like to do to other parts of his body.

His Adam's apple bobbed. His body froze. And the playful look in his eyes disappeared.

Flashing a glance that screamed *Yes!* she circled her tongue around his thumb, then slowly sucked it down until her lips met the pad of his palm. Then she reversed the motion, easing back and dragging her tongue along the flesh all the way. His fingers caressed her cheek, but his eyes never left her mouth. They stayed captivated by her, and she knew by the look in them he'd gone hard as a rock. She could feel it in the stillness of the moment.

She was driving him crazy. He'd gone rigid as stone, not a muscle in his body moving as she stroked and sucked, the air getting hotter with every taste.

She loved this feeling of power, knowing that she was toying with something that could erupt with an intensity she'd only sensed in her dreams. He was fixated on her, the room devoid of everything but her lips making unspoken promises of undeniable pleasure.

And just when she began to consider moving on to better things, he cupped her face with both hands, shot out an expletive and crushed his mouth to hers.

7

OKAY, SO MAYBE toying with Carly had been a bad idea. In fact, now that he thought about it, it was about the stupidest thing he'd ever done, only to be surpassed by what he planned to do next.

He hadn't expected things to turn out like this. He was supposed to tease her, make her squirm a bit about the survey, raise a few flags of concern before he dropped the bomb that he knew what she'd done. Right about now he was supposed to be scolding her, not running his hands through her hair and shoving his tongue down her throat.

But that's exactly where this had gone, and damn if he could find it in him to change course now.

He should have known that taunting Carly was a bad idea. From the moment he'd walked into Hall Technologies two years ago she'd been the forbidden fruit he couldn't ignore. And like twisting a crank on a child's mechanical toy, every month that went by had only strung him tighter. Her bright smile would turn the crank one notch, her throaty laugh another. Calming words, the way she hummed when she worked, the scintillating cleavage—twist, twist, twist. By the time this survey came around, he'd been wound so tight a wink might have caused him to snap. How he thought he could pull off a fake seduction and keep his pants on was a blunder for the ages. Carly calling his bluff had been one turn too many, and with the wheels set in motion, he had no idea where it would land.

He laced his fingers through her hair and drove the kiss deeper. She tasted like sweet peach tea, smelled clean as fresh lemons, and with skin soft as a buttercup, he wouldn't be calling a halt anytime soon. His first sampling of Carly Abrams was what he'd both feared and expected, and without the will to put on the brakes, he surrendered to dig in and enjoy the ride.

Their lips still locked, she slipped off her chair and onto his lap, hiking the skirt up her thighs and straddling him with two long, smooth legs. The move freed his hands to explore all those delicious curves and valleys, and it wasn't long before he found his way up her shirt and over those two luscious mounds.

She groaned. He hardened. She inched farther up his thighs and his cock stiffened more. He wondered how hard it would be to unzip his jeans and slide inside her, but with condoms in his back pocket and two bodies on one unsteady office chair, he didn't dare risk it.

Squeezing her breasts in his hands, he pulled his mouth away and whispered, "We need to move."

Those turquoise eyes had darkened, her lips had puffed and reddened from the stubble on his jaw, and while she went to work unbuttoning his shirt, she asked, "Does the door really lock?"

He bit the sensitive flesh under her chin. "There's a dead bolt."

She pulled open his shirt and stroked her hands across his chest. "We can really do this."

Working his way up to one tender earlobe, he replied, "We can do anything you want, sweetheart."

He skimmed his hands down her legs and slipped them up

under her skirt, and she hissed when his thumbs reached the soft curls of her sex. He'd barely grazed the edge of her panties before the slick heat welcomed him, and his stiff cock twitched from the rush sweeping through him. Only moments into this, she was already hot, ripe and ready, and he sank his teeth into the base of her neck, needing to turn his focus away from the place that could tip him too early.

He'd wanted Carly too badly for too long, and her eagerness to push things further wasn't helping his restraint. He hadn't expected any of this. He hadn't really thought that underneath the cheery schoolgirl a fiery siren lay in waiting, nor had he thought her staunch animosity toward him could peel away so easily. Yet here they were, poised to play out every fantasy that had haunted him since the day they'd met, and damned if he could hear a voice inside telling him not to.

He wanted her so much it hurt. He ached to soak in a piece of that sweet sunshine she carried around with her and he throbbed to explore the fiery woman he'd exposed. It wasn't desire so much as hard, painful hunger, and when she slid her tongue under the curve of his jaw, he almost feared the deep sensations running through him.

Something about it felt too right, and, whipping his hands up from under her skirt, he wrapped his arms around her waist and squeezed, feeling an unexplainable need to hold her tight and close.

Her response was a delightful gasp and the breathy suggestion that they take this party to the couch. She slid off his lap and held out a hand, and Matt was miles from arguing. Pulling out of the chair, he stepped to the door and flicked the switch to the dead bolt, turning back to her just in time to watch her skirt drop to the floor.

Without an ounce of hesitation, she crisscrossed her hands over the hem of her shirt and pulled it over her head, leaving her standing by one stuffy chair, her long, slim body clad only in a pale cream bra and matching silk panties.

He nearly choked on his tongue. Carly Abrams in the flesh was more beautiful than his fantasies. Dark, silky hair contrasted sharply against skin the color of cream, and her blue eyes nearly shimmered with expectation. She stood neither confident nor ashamed, simply offering herself for display, and Matt found the unassuming stance about as sexy as they come.

Puffing out a faint cough, he cleared his throat before choking out, "Are you trying to kill me?"

A deliciously evil smile curved one side of her mouth. "Maybe I am."

"You're off to a good start."

Reaching behind her, she unclasped her bra and let it drop to her feet, exposing two perfectly beautiful breasts, and Matt clasped his hands into fists to keep from reaching out and groping them like a schoolboy.

"How's this?" she asked, and when he didn't answer, she slipped out of her panties and stood naked before him, a pair of black heeled sandals the only clothing left on her body.

When she moved to kick one off, he shot out, "Don't!" and she raised a brow of intrigue, opting to stop and wait, her gaze telling him the rest was up to him.

And Matt couldn't decide where to start. There were too many options. The most desirable was to plop her down on the chair, swing those luscious heeled legs over his shoulders and bury himself in oblivion.

And thirty seconds later the whole encounter would be over.

So instead he opted for plan B, one of several fantasies he'd had starring Carly since he'd taken a peek at those survey questions. Given that's what had started this whole thing, he might as well find out if any of those answers were true. The fact that she stood there so unabashedly exposed left him suspecting she hadn't lied about everything, and if so, he was about to have his best day on the job to date.

Slowly he strolled toward her, savoring the look of anticipation on her face, knowing he had the power to fulfill her expectations. He wasn't a cocky lover for nothing, and if he was risking rumor spreading through the office, he intended it to be in his favor.

He snaked a hand around her waist and pulled her against him, and though she parted her lips, expecting a kiss, he simply held her close and stared.

"I intend to make sure you like this," he said.

Tugging his shirt off his shoulders, she replied, "I'd like it better if you were naked, too."

He allowed his shirt to drop, but when she reached for his trousers, he held her hands. "That time will come."

A soft pout formed on her face and the shot of affection made him want to kiss it away. Miss-Sunshine-turned-fiery-vixen had a playful side, and as he eased her down on one of the chairs, he wondered how many more sides there were to this mystery package.

Kneeling in front of her, he spread her legs wide. "Don't worry. Neither of us will go away unsatisfied." Then he clasped his mouth to her breast.

She arched her back and moaned, and just as he'd wanted, the playful pout drained away to something sensual. He spent a short time sampling her breasts, licking the taut coral nipples, trailing a line down her waist so close to her sex she gasped before he turned and went back the way he came. He wanted to drive her crazy for him, to make her crave him as badly as he'd craved her. And when they were done, he wanted her to think of him as the best lover she'd ever had.

Because he wanted to be the best lover she'd ever had.

Her fingernails scraped his back, pushing more blood to his cock before its time. Holding off wouldn't be easy, but he had no intention of sating his needs until he'd watched her crumble beneath him.

Again he trailed his mouth down her torso, teasing the flesh at her opening before trolling back up, and when he dipped a third time, he allowed his tongue to scrape between the slick heat of her folds.

The sweetness nearly pushed him over. The rush of breath to her lungs sucked the air from the room. And when she wriggled down in a gesture of offering, he denied her and turned away.

She let out a grunt of frustration, and he smiled.

"Did you like that?" he asked.

Her response was an agonizing, "Yes."

"Do you want to come, baby?"

"I want you to fuck me," she said, the statement so sexually out of character his cock nearly shot free of his slacks.

"I think you need to come first." And backing up the demand, he spread her and placed his mouth right where it mattered most.

A squeak slipped from her throat, and her legs began to tremble as Matt slipped his tongue over her clit and the slick flesh around it. He ached to push a finger inside to see how tight she was, but he was already at the edge. Any more surprises from Carly would ruin the great run he'd started, so instead he caressed her thighs while he brought her to the edge of orgasm.

She whispered out words of warning he didn't need to hear. He already knew she was close. He could feel her clit swelling against his tongue, could taste the sweet slickness from her core as the scent of arousal swarmed his nose. She was almost there, and knowing how much more he had planned, he didn't hesitate to let her come fast and hard against his mouth.

Slim fingers slid through his hair, then grasped tightly as she sucked in a breath and exhaled a silent release. Her nub convulsed against his tongue, and he took it into his mouth and suckled it while he clasped his hands to her hips to hold her steady. He could tell she wanted to cry out, the low rumblings from her chest leaking sounds of desperate silence.

And when she finally calmed, he looked up to see her head tilted back against the chair, her sated eyes staring at the ceiling and her chest heaving in an effort to restore her breath. He loved the sight, the look of a satisfied woman, an expression numb from climax.

He intended to see it again.

Rising up and bringing his lips back to one delicate ear, he smiled and whispered, "Now I can fuck you."

THE MERE SOUND of Matt's voice using the very naughty and highly un-office-like phrase sent Carly climbing back up the slope of arousal all over again.

Never in her life had she stripped for a man and stood naked before him—most definitely not in the office—but something about the way he'd looked at her, had devoured her in that chair and had savored her with his mouth, hands and eyes left her feeling bold and empowered. At that moment he could have told her to put on a wig and dance the jitterbug and she would have given it her best shot.

She wondered if he knew he had that power over her.

The rattle of something strange caught her attention, and she looked down to see Matt sifting through a basket of stress toys, then coming up with an object about the size of a tennis ball. He threaded a small loop on one end around his two middle fingers, allowing the ball to cradle in his palm.

When she opened her mouth to inquire, he snapped a switch, and the resulting hum answered her impending question.

"What is that, a vibrator?"

"A handheld massager I've had ideas about for quite a while now."

She stifled an excited grin, not wanting to look overeager but having a hard time pulling it off. For a long time now she'd wanted sex that was exciting, so much so that she'd gone out on this limb in the belief that Matt might be the one to provide it.

It looked as though her instincts had been correct.

Digging through the basket, he brought out another and tossed it to her, and her excitement waned. She wasn't sure what to do with it, and with things starting off on such a great high, she feared her inexperience would ruin it for them both.

She'd always suspected Matt had a taste for wild and experienced women, ones who knew their way around a man's body and the kinds of things that turned men on. Carly wasn't that kind of woman, and if he'd expected her to be, he might be headed for disappointment.

Swallowing a gulp of nerves, she slipped the massager around her fingers as Matt had done and waited as he pulled a condom from his wallet, tossed it on her belly, then yanked down his trousers. One thick cock sprang out, and he edged in closer and jutted his chin toward the foil pack.

"Put it on me, babe."

Her eyes wide, she tried to will the jitters from her fingers. She'd never put a condom on a man before and prayed there wasn't a trick to it, but she wasn't about to confess that to him. She wanted to shed the Sally Sunshine image that always seemed to keep men like him away, so with the toy still cupped to one hand, she worked to tear open the foil packet while Matt held his cock in waiting.

Tugging out the latex sheath, she let the packet drop to the floor before she unrolled the condom over his shaft without incident, feeling the tiny thrill of victory as he proceeded in obvious assumption that none of this was new to her.

But it was. Every moment of it was. From the instant she'd climbed on his lap and sunk her tongue deep in his mouth she'd been marking new ground. She'd never been this bold, had never risked having sex in a place where she could end up caught and in trouble, had never had sex with her shoes on and most definitely had never played with toys, much less on the very first time.

He was the man of her fantasies, all right, and just like her greatest fantasy, she ached with anticipation over what would come next.

Flicking the switch on her massager, the light hum vibrated in her hand, and she looked to follow Matt's lead. He slowly trailed his up her thigh, letting the smooth tickling sensation heighten her arousal. He sank it into the apex of her thigh, lightly grazed it over her mound before moving it down the other side, the vibration curling her toes and reawakening her already-sated sex.

Guiding her hand to her thigh, he said, "Put it where it feels good," before taking his own and massaging it around the base of his shaft and behind his balls.

His cock jerked and his eyes rolled, and Carly followed suit, experimenting with her own vibrating ball. If Matt was sexy simply walking around the office, he was lethal in the flesh. His chiseled chest was deliciously rugged, a faint dusting of hair trickling down in a line over taut abs and disappearing around his navel. His erection drove her mad with anticipation, the deep look of pleasure on that handsome face nearly bringing her to tears. They watched each other, studying one another's motions, before Matt nudged them to trade positions, and she guided her ball around his shaft, the hard feel of his flesh exciting her, pulsing between her legs as he lolled his head to the side and soaked in the sensation.

"This is good," he moaned, then edged farther between her legs until the tender tip of his shaft was positioned for entry.

"Scoot down," he said, and she obliged, her heart racing to see where this would lead, how he would feel inside her, and with her hips teetering on the edge of the chair, he slid inside.

Her body stretched for him, her ball still tickling the base of his shaft, and she arched to take him in deeper, his resulting groan heating her blood and adding vigor to her moves. Between the erection stroking her core and the oscillations fluttering between them, she was headed for another hard and searing climax, and the look in Matt's eyes said he wasn't far behind.

They stroked and moved together, using the balls to tantalize the area around their thighs and the space where they joined, and when Matt bent in to suckle her breasts, a rising wave began to crest between her legs.

"I'm going to come," she whispered, prompting him to increase the pressure of the massager between her legs.

She squirmed and tried to move away, not wanting it to

happen so fast, but he simply moved with her and took up the space.

"Go, baby," he said.

"Not yet."

"Yes, now," he urged, stroking his ball closer to her clit. Cupping her hand in his, he pushed her ball down under them, guiding them both to add sensation she didn't need. She was going to boil over, and when he slipped out a curse and thrust faster, she knew he was on the cusp, too.

"Oh," he groaned, then he groaned it again, his breath growing heavy, his eyes closing and beads of sweat forming on his brow. He hissed in a breath; she could see him struggling to hold on. And with one more pass between them, she dropped her ball on the chair next to her and split apart.

The climax came deep and heavy, ripping through her chest and squeezing in her throat. She bit her lip to stay quiet, but a low squeak escaped her, and when they couldn't take more, Matt dropped his ball, closed his lips over hers and grunted his climax into her throat.

His tongue shot into her mouth, aching moans following in its wake while he jerked and buckled against her. It seemed to go on forever, his body consuming her from head to toe, drinking her in, capturing her breath until every inch of them moved, breathed and pulsed as one.

Pulling his lips from hers, he expelled a long, luxurious breath at the nape of her neck, and she dug her fingers into his ass and pulled him close, wanting their joining to last just a little longer.

"You were amazing," he said after a very long moment, his voice raspy and tired.

She sat for a moment, staring at the ceiling, enjoying the

hard feel of him over her body, the occasional twitch of his cock inside her and the heavy thump of his heart against her breast.

"There's plenty more to be had," she said, already fully deciding that this wouldn't be their only time if she had her way.

He lifted from her grasp, stood up and pulled his pants around his waist, using a nearby box of tissue to discard the remnants of the condom before tossing it in the trash. The sated look on his face had begun to fade as he searched for his shirt, and a sudden shift in the air had her reaching for her own clothing, the need to cover up coming over her without explanation.

Had that not been the right thing to say?

"Or not," she quickly slipped in.

He caught the snap to her tone and glanced over. His reluctant expression prompted her to dress even faster. He had *Dear Jane* written all over his face, and if she was going to hear that the best sex of her life had been a mistake, she would at least do it clothed.

"Look, Carly," he started, but she held up a hand, not interested in hearing the rest. Just the tone of those two words said it all. It was the start of a speech about what had just happened, how she shouldn't misunderstand, how she shouldn't read more into the situation than what it was, him being a guy like him and her a woman like her.

No way would she listen to that.

"Don't wreck a great one-night stand," she said. "I get it. I'm a big girl. Let's just forget this happened and move on."

His eyes widened. "That's not where I was going."

She hurriedly slipped her skirt up, but the hem got caught in her heel and she heard the dreaded sound of fabric tearing.

Sex with her shoes on. Brilliant.

"I'd definitely like more where that came from," he went

on as she pulled her heel from the hem and lifted her skirt to her waist. "We just need to keep this under wraps is all."

She stopped and stared. "What do you think I'm going to do—walk out of this room and tell everyone we just had sex?"

He shrugged as though the answer to that question might actually have been yes.

Her jaw dropped. "You really think I'd do that."

His jaw bobbed. "No… Yes… I mean, you get around."

She shot out a squeak. "What's *that* supposed to mean?"

He stared at the floor and took a long breath, and that's when Carly stopped looking. Instead she rushed to throw together the last of her clothing before she slapped him.

"Not what it sounded like," he said. "I mean, you've got a lot of friends here, and I think it would be best if this didn't get spread around the office."

Smoothing her hands over her skirt, then going to work on her hair, she held back the flames and tried to speak calmly.

It didn't work.

"Trust me—I won't be telling anyone I had sex with *you*."

Now it was his turn to gape. "What's *that* supposed to mean?"

"Exactly how it sounded," she snapped. "You don't have to worry about this happening again or anyone hearing about the one time it did." Moving to the door, she flipped open the dead bolt and reached for the handle. "As far as I'm concerned, this is already forgotten."

And with that, she stormed out the door.

8

MATT SLID ON HIS batting helmet, tightened the gloves at his wrists and flicked on the pitching machine before grasping his favorite Louisville Slugger tightly around the grip. With his eye on the machine, the distant sounds around him began to fade. Besides the *thwoop-thwoop* of the pitches in the neighboring cages, there was the tinny smack of a ball making contact with an aluminum bat, the constant creak of the old wood floor in the two-story warehouse and the low murmur of conversation. The sounds were old and familiar to him, comforting as a lullaby in this place that was more a home to him than the tiny boathouse he'd grown up in.

The light on the machine turned from red to yellow, and he shifted his weight to his back leg, holding the bat well over his shoulder as he waited for the pitch.

It came high and outside for a swing and a miss.

He curled his lip, tapped the bat on home plate, then readied his stance for the next pitch. The scents of rubber, oil and dust filled his nostrils, and he took them in, soaking them up like a stiff shot of whiskey to calm his nerves. He'd been hanging out at the Dugout since he was old enough to make the two-mile ride on his bicycle from home. More times than he could count he'd gotten in trouble for staying here past dark, time getting away from him as he chugged back Dr

Peppers and spilled his troubles to Stuey Callebrew, the Dugout's owner.

Since Matt was about seven, Stuey had been more of a father to him than his own dad after Matt's parents divorced and Jeff Jacobs turned his attention to his new wife and family. Matt would be a liar if he said Stu had been an adequate stand-in for his own dad. There hadn't been much Stu could do to take away the sting of being tossed out like yesterday's news. But over the years Matt had grown to love him and had begun to consider this place his real home.

The next pitch came tight inside, and Matt ducked and turned out of habit, nearly spinning himself off his heels.

Someday Matt was going to buy Stu a new set of machines.

The next two pitches were high and wide, and Matt hadn't done more than foul-tip either one. Frustration welled in his gut. He wanted the rush, the warmth of victory when ball meets bat square in the sweet spot and goes sailing over that imaginary outfield wall. Sex was barely better than the feel of standing at home plate after hearing that special smack only home-run balls made. Not to mention the crowd holding a collective breath as they all strained to get a glimpse of a shot destined for the center-field bleachers.

It was in those moments that Matt had won. He could do more than good enough, he'd be the best. No one could tell him how to make that shot any better because nothing was ever better than a home-run ball.

The pitch came in over the top, and Matt tipped it into the netting, slamming his bat on home plate for not taking good advantage of a well-pitched baseball.

"Lady trouble, huh?" Stu Callebrew spoke with a drawl even though he was born and raised in Modesto.

Matt stepped back in the batter's box and prepared for the pitch. "What makes you say that?"

"You're reaching. You always reach when the ladies get you down. You pull the ball left when your mother drives you crazy. You swing at the inside when it's work. And when things are going well, I don't see you at all."

Matt blinked, and the ball sped by, hitting the chest-high backstop with a pop. "You think you know me that well?"

Stu slipped his fingers through the chain-link fence and smiled, his sun-worn face wrinkling up at the corners of his eyes and making ripples in his forehead. "Am I wrong?"

No, Stu wasn't wrong. When it came to Matt, Stu was always on the money. But Matt wasn't in the mood to spill his guts today. After all, what would he say?

Well, you see, Stu, I've got this beautiful woman I've been eyeing for two years now. Yesterday I got the chance to screw her silly in the project room at the office. She was every man's fantasy and the best sex I've had since I can remember. Problem is, the minute it was over, I opened my mouth, said the wrong thing—and now she won't talk to me.

Oh, yeah, and we're supposed to be teaming up on a project together, so I've messed up my career in the process, as well.

Another day, another episode in the life of Matt Michael Jacobs, world's best screwup.

The pitch came up fast, and Matt stifled the impulse to swing, wanting to prove Stu wrong about his reaching theory. But when the next one came out in the same spot, he caught himself swinging.

And Stu threw his head back and roared with laughter.

"Glad I can entertain you," Matt grumbled, then winced at the tone, knowing what he'd get in response.

"Feeling sorry for ourselves today, are we?"

"I'm not. I can't speak for you," he lied.

The pitch came in low and straight, and Matt hit a high blooper back to the machine.

He knew better than to let on that he had lost himself in pity. Stu had started his career as a coach at Fresno before opening up the Dugout in Marin, and the one thing he'd never put up with was a player feeling sorry for himself. Stu knew that if he allowed one player to whine, it would run through the club like a bad epidemic. Pity was for losers, he'd say, and he'd meant it. He hadn't even allowed Matt to lick his wounds when his father had skipped his college graduation or his Anaheim draft party or any of the other important events in his life because his stepmother, Barbara, wouldn't allow it. Barbara was needy and insecure, never getting over the fact that she hadn't given Jeff Jacobs his firstborn child. She'd spent the bulk of their marriage trying to make him forget Matt existed, and for the most part she'd succeeded.

Back when Matt was a scrappy kid taking his rejection out on the world, Stu had had more patience, but the older Matt got, the less Stu accepted Matt's self-defeating attitude. Matt supposed Stu was the reason he'd made as much of his life as he had. Someone had to draw the line and set boundaries. God knows his mother certainly hadn't, the woman so embittered by her ex, she'd never given Matt so much as a stern word. But on days like today Matt just wanted to be left alone with his misery and he was quickly beginning to realize seeking solace in the Dugout might have been a bad idea.

"Well, I'm doing good today," Stu said, sarcastically adding, "Thanks for asking."

The ball came in fast and straight, and Matt stepped out of

the batter's box, letting it smack into the backstop right about at Stu's knees. The man pulled his hands from the fence in time to avoid getting pinched.

"Oh, sorry about that." Matt grinned.

"You're a sorry one all right."

The easy banter between the two was already lifting Matt's mood. He'd wanted to stop thinking about Carly, mostly because he'd accepted the fact there was nothing he could do about the situation he'd created. Despite his attempt at smoothing things over between them, she'd given him the cold shoulder all day, staying businesslike and professional but not gracing him with any pleasantries. She'd drawn a symbolic circle around herself and ordered him not to cross it, and he didn't need to hear the words to get the hint. What they'd had was a one-time incident that wouldn't be repeated, and just as she'd said when she left the lab the day before, she'd moved on and forgotten about it.

Now all Matt had to do was the same.

Easier said than done.

"So are you going to tell me her name?" Stu asked.

He absently replied, "Carly," before realizing Stu had tricked him into talking.

"She must be special if she's brought you here. How come I haven't met her?"

"She's just a woman I work with."

"Hmm. But you're reaching wide right, which means the problem's more pleasure than business."

"It's both," he said, popping another high fly. *Easy out.*

"That explains why you can't hit *anything* today."

Against his will, a smile broke one corner of Matt's mouth. Damn, he loved Stu. The man always knew how to get him out of a funk, mostly by not putting up with any BS. If it was sympathy, hand-holding and coddling Matt wanted, he could seek out his mother, but he'd grown up enough these last few years to learn the poor-me attitude got him nothing more than a pink slip and a one-way plane ticket home. This time around, he was going to the Stu Callebrew school of wisdom, where to get ahead in life you worked hard, sucked it up and let your mistakes be a lesson, not an excuse.

And the lesson he'd learned this time around was to stop thinking he and Carly could someday see eye to eye and to never, ever play with fire. At least where beautiful women were concerned.

"It's nothing I can't get over," Matt said, and it was true. Having sex with Carly had been high on his list of stupid moves, but it didn't look as though she intended to destroy his life over it. Now he just needed to forget their encounter and get back to business—a feat not easy but certainly manageable. All he had to do was somehow erase the taste of her from his lips or her scent from his nostrils or the memory of her body in his arms and around his cock or the sound of her moans—

How much did a good lobotomy cost these days? he wondered.

"Ouch," Stu said. "That sounds like you're the one who got turned down."

"Open one mouth, insert one pair of size-thirteen cleats." Readying himself for the pitch, he shifted his weight and stood focused.

And the fastball sailed past him.

He stepped out of the box and kicked the inside of his sneaker with the tip of his bat. "Every time I'm around this woman I can't seem to say the right thing. This last time it got me in more trouble than usual, but she seems to be moving past it. Now I've just got to do the same."

Stu responded with a wide mouse-eating grin, and Matt frowned. "I'm glad you find that amusing."

"I'm glad you've finally found someone special."

Matt blinked. "I must have been talking to your bum ear, Stu. The woman hates me. And if she wasn't so damned sexy, I'd hate her, too."

It was a bald-faced lie, but Matt said it anyway. Truth was, he admired the hell out of Carly. She had that spark of something special that made people love her, and it wasn't just the favors she did. It was something magical, something completely elusive to a guy like Matt, who always had to work hard to keep a friend and even then failed more often than he succeeded. Matt would do anything for anyone who asked him, too, but people rarely asked. It was as if he walked around with *Leave me alone* tattooed on his forehead, and for the life of him he didn't know how he got it or how to make it go away. It was just there, part of his being, his soul.

The next ball came in square, and he tipped it back to the machine, not even really trying anymore. Being honest with himself, he hadn't come here looking for the thrill of a solid shot, he'd come here to talk to Stu, and this was the way they'd always communicated. Stu wasn't his dad, so Matt had never felt right about coming up and flat-out asking for his ear, but Stu knew Matt better than anyone. He read the signs and always came around when Matt needed to talk. It was like a little dance. When Matt needed a friend, he'd show up at the cages and start swinging a bat until Stu got him talking about his troubles. And like the father-friend he was, Stu always made things better.

"Well, I know not to try and teach you anything about

women, what with me and Leonora married thirty-seven years and you so successful with *your* love life."

Matt smirked at the slam.

"I just happen to think *hate*'s a pretty strong word," Stu added. "And when people start using strong words, it's usually because there's some strong feelings underneath."

"Sure, like animosity, ire, frustration, competition. We've got all that going on." He twirled the bat in a circle and stepped out of the box. "In fact, now that you've made me think about it, we're practically perfect for each other."

Stu laughed and Matt smiled as he stepped in for the pitch. This time he hit it square into the painted mural of an outfield filled with fans Stu had commissioned about a dozen years ago. Netting kept the balls from actually smacking into it, but the sentiment was the same. You hit the ball into the far wall net and you'd just hit a home run.

"See? You start telling the truth and things shift in your favor," Stu pointed out.

Matt hit three more like it, not really wanting Stu to be right but enjoying it nonetheless. This was exactly what he'd needed—to get out of the condo, blow off some steam and go back to the office tomorrow with a clear head and a new attitude. He'd accomplished the first three and he knew before he left here tonight he'd accomplish the last, as well.

"Hey, while you're here, I've got something I want you to do for me," Stu said.

"Shoot."

"I got a kid I want you to work with. He could use some help with his swing."

Matt stepped away from the plate and flicked off the machine. He found it odd Stu was asking him to help with the kids. Back in high school, he'd liked working with them, remembering the days when he was a scrawny tyke himself and one of the older players paid him extra attention. Given his natural talent with a baseball, he'd gotten a lot of that, and it had become somewhat of a rite of passage to take the younger kids under his wing when he was in the mood and had the time. A side of him had thought Stu might ask him to help out now that he'd moved back to town, and when he hadn't, Matt had never asked why.

He'd been afraid of the answer.

He'd already been told by the Scottsdale Sidewinders he wasn't good enough to move up from the Nationals' AA team, and his agent had been told the same by a half dozen more teams. When he'd come home defeated, he hadn't wanted to hear that Stu thought he wasn't good enough to work with the kids anymore, either, even though he'd never truly believed it. But given the gravity of his disappointment back then, he hadn't been able to risk any more knocks, so he simply never went there.

But he could go there now.

"I thought you were through asking me to coach," he commented.

Stu hung his hands on the fence and smiled. "No one's ever through coaching, son. Sometimes you need to take a break, though."

"And when I came home, you felt I needed a break?"

Stu's tired eyes looked at Matt with all seriousness. "Sometimes when a man takes a hit, the best thing is to get right back on the horse. Other times it's best to stay away for a while." Nodding, he added, "You needed to step away for a while."

"So why the turnaround now?"

Stu shrugged and cocked his head. "I think you're ready."

Matt twirled the bat in his hand, a nervous habit he'd had since he was a kid. He wasn't sure what to think of Stu's words, but in his maturity he'd learned that Stu was right more times than he was wrong. In fact, Matt couldn't ever remember Stu being wrong about anything.

"This kid," Stu said. "He's cocky."

Matt raised a brow. "So you instantly thought of me."

"Yep. He also thinks I'm too old to know anything about baseball. He'll probably think you're too old, too. But he's got good focus and good instincts. He just has some mechanical problems, and if he'd get over that hump of doing something that doesn't feel natural for a minute, we could retrain his bad habits."

"Let me take a crack at him," Matt offered.

"He's ten," Stu said as if that might make Matt change his mind. They both knew that was a tough age. If the boy had started in T-ball, he already had five years of bad habits to break. If he was cocky, that meant he was probably better than most and didn't think he needed the help. And if he was ten, that meant he was heading for middle school and some of the toughest years of a young boy's life.

Exactly the kind of challenge Matt needed to get his mind off the mess he'd made of his working relationship with Carly.

He flashed Stu a knowing smile. "You're giving me this kid on purpose, aren't you?"

"Yes, I'm tired of the whining."

"Are you talking about me or the kid?"

Snapping a wink, Stu backed away from the cage and headed toward the pro shop. "Yes."

9

"I NEED THOSE presentation materials. Have you finished up the slide show yet?"

Matt's smooth, quiet voice slid over Carly's shoulders like raw silk. It seemed no matter how angry she wanted to be with him, her body kept responding to the slightest of gestures. Even with her back to him and her eyes on some very gnarly looking HTML code, the mere sound of his voice slipped down around her waist and tingled at the apex of her thighs.

And the vivid memory of his hard, naked body plunging her into euphoria wasn't helping one bit.

Shaking the scene from her thoughts for the umpteenth time, she replied, "I e-mailed it to you a half hour ago."

She hadn't intended the clipped tone. It had simply become her normal voice around him since their interlude in the lab and that lame apology he'd attempted in the hall later that day.

The apology you didn't deserve.

Now there was another thing keeping her nerves on edge. That stupid voice in her head, the one that kept trying to tell her she'd overreacted and that *she* should be the one offering *him* apologies. She really didn't need it. She'd gone over and over the incident more times than she wanted to admit and she always came to the conclusion she'd had every right to be mad. So mad she would stay, voices or no voices.

"Aren't you being a little hard on him?"

Okay, now the voices are just getting creepy.

Blinking, she looked up and saw Bev hanging over her cubicle wall.

"Huh?" She glanced back and saw that Matt had walked off.

"I said, weren't you being a little harsh? You practically bit his head off."

Carly frowned. "He needs to learn to check his e-mail." That way he'd stop having reason to come by her desk and ask her questions in that sultry tone while wafting that darned aftershave around her cubicle, where it seemed to linger all day. At least this time she hadn't had to look at him. He was probably wearing those worn, rugged boots today, the ones with the buckles at the ankles that made him look all sexy, like a young Clint Eastwood in one of those spaghetti Westerns.

Bev lowered her voice. "He doesn't deserve the treatment you're giving him. From what you told me, all he did was ask you not to spread *it* around."

"That was offensive. I wouldn't have told a soul."

"You told me within minutes of leaving the room."

"You're different. You don't count."

"You've told a half dozen other people what a jerk he is."

"But I never said why."

"It doesn't matter. People are still beginning to talk."

Carly's frown deepened into a pout. She hated logic when she felt like being illogical. It was the party pooper crashing her misery gala, and she'd been having a good time wallowing in her self-inflicted pain.

Bev held up her wallet. "I'm going for coffee. Come on."

Carly let out a long breath and rose from her seat, knowing

she was about to get a block-long lecture from Bev and, worse, knowing she deserved it. She was being irrationally testy, punishing Matt from the moment he'd climaxed and failed to look dreamily into her eyes and profess his everlasting love for her.

Of course, that wasn't what she'd consciously expected him to do, but after she'd considered that awkward postsex moment, she'd surmised that was about the only thing he could have done to avoid the reaction he got. Because when he'd gotten up and started gathering his clothes, Carly had discovered something very important about herself.

She was not a just-for-fun-fling kinda gal.

She'd been trying to deny it for days, telling herself that Matt's insensitivity was the cause of the wrangling nerves nestled in her stomach. She'd hoped to convince herself that she could be free and loose, a cosmopolitan woman having wild, flippant sex square in the middle of her office and not expect anything more from a man.

But when she shoveled her own garbage away, she realized it was all a lie. Truth was, as much as she craved a hot sexual thrill, she craved loving affection more, and as the two women stepped through the double glass doors and out into the late-afternoon sun, Carly tried not to groan. Apparently, she did belong with nice, steady men who bored her to tears in bed. At least she'd never stormed out on any of them, and when the act was done, none of them had felt compelled to tell her to keep her mouth shut.

"I know what you're going to say," she said, holding up a hand before Bev could open her mouth. "I went over the deep end."

"I wouldn't go *that* far. What did he say? *You get around?* Not exactly the words of a prince."

"He's never been very graceful with words. I should have figured that out by now."

And honestly, it wasn't how he'd said it but that he'd seen through her so easily that touched a hot nerve. When she'd sat basking in the aftermath of the two best orgasms of her life, she *had* wanted to run out and scream it to the world, and Matt's comment had made it painfully evident he hadn't felt the same way.

He'd made the truth between them obvious. To a girl like Carly, sex was intimate and special. To a guy like Matt, sex was sex. She couldn't deny who she really was. Sally Sunshine. Mary Quite Contrary. The little good girl who'd tried to take a walk on the wild side but couldn't even round the first lap. She was a fake, a fraud and, worse than anything else, Matt had called her bluff before he'd even pulled his pants on.

Yes, she was definitely that pathetic. Contrary to the wild sex puppet she'd envisioned she could be, reality proved she was completely inept at carrying out a casual tryst, and when Matt had pointed that out in his offhanded way, she'd lashed out by making him the bad guy.

The two women stood at the corner next to the Happy Lantern restaurant, waiting for the light to change.

"Listen, be mad at him all you want," Bev said. "And unless you want to get him back in the sack, I wouldn't lose sleep over what's come down between you two. I'm only saying you've got to lighten up on the I-hate-Matt campaign. Like I said, people are starting to talk. And, in case you've forgotten, thanks to your own scheme, you two are supposed to be the ideal couple."

"According to a stupid survey."

"According to our biggest client that you need to impress if you want that promotion."

When the signal changed, they stepped across the street on their way down the block to Lone Dog Coffee, and Carly let Bev's words and the breezy air clear her mind. Bev was right. She really did need to let it go, if for no other reason than to take back the control she'd surrendered that afternoon. Matt wasn't worth the energy she'd been pouring into hating him, and Bev's reminder was exactly the reality check she needed.

Get her head on straight, forget about him and go back to the task of showing management how ideal she was for that team lead position.

"Of course," Bev added, "given what you told me about your encounter, I wouldn't rule out trying to get Matt back in the sack."

Carly huffed and shook her head. "I think I've humiliated myself enough for one lifetime, thank you. Besides, I'm not cut out for the casual tryst."

"That's ridiculous. Of course you're cut out for casual trysts. Have you forgotten Marty Pritchard?"

"I'm trying to." Marty Pritchard was a corporate event planner down in the peninsula who liked to call her up when business brought him north of San Francisco. Though the man had never given her two cosmic orgasms like those she'd shared with Matt, he was okay—*okay* being the operative word. Her heart had never ached watching Marty walk out the door, mostly because she wasn't interested enough and he wasn't good enough to make her pine for something more. In fact, timing was the best thing Marty had going for him. He always seemed to call when she had nothing to do, and a quick dinner and a romp in the hay sounded better than reruns of *Friends*.

Matt Jacobs was a different story. He was the type of man she'd yearn for something more with, and even if he were apt to give it to her, she knew without a doubt playing around with him would lead to one heavy heartache. His survey hadn't lied. It had painted a clear picture of a man wrong for her in every way that counted, and no matter how badly she wanted to ignore that fact and enjoy him for the sex, she simply couldn't separate her emotions where he was concerned.

The sex was too good, the man was too wrong. It was as simple as that. And if she wanted to keep her career intact and her heart in one piece, she'd need to keep her distance from Matt Jacobs.

MATT CONNECTED his laptop to the wall monitor so he could test the presentation materials before his and Carly's meeting with Brayton and Andy. With a hum, his CD drive whirred on and the display on his laptop came to life on the flat-screen monitor mounted on the far wall of the company's main conference room. Clicking through the screens, he took a moment to add final touches to the materials Carly had put together, adjusting an occasional font or modifying a screen transition to give the overall presentation more flair.

Though Carly had brought good insights to the project, her presentation skills tended to be too primitive for his taste, getting the point across but lacking the dazzle Matt had learned impressed clients. It was funny, really, how the most difficult and complicated programming tasks seemed to go unnoticed, but add a dancing bear or dissolve the screen into a shimmer of shooting stars and clients marveled at the results.

And Matt was determined to invoke a lot of marvel when it came to this project. Whatever he had to do to land this management job, he'd do it. If it was impressing Hall with another project well done, then he'd hand it over with all the glitz and chutzpah that satisfied clients. That part was easy. The hard part was getting into Hall's head to see exactly what kind of plan he was brewing and how likely a candidate Matt really was in taking on this new team.

For days he'd been waiting for the right moment to broach the subject with Hall, but so far the opportunity hadn't come up. And though Matt could be patient, he didn't want Hall to sink too far into any decisions without the chance to throw out a few ideas or sway the vote in his favor.

"Setting up early, as usual."

Matt turned to find Brayton Hall standing in the doorway clad in Friday blue jeans and a pink button-down shirt he couldn't quite pull off.

"Yes," Matt said. "I don't like dealing with surprises while the client's waiting."

Brayton stepped across the threshold, pulled back a chair and took a seat. Maybe this would be the opportunity Matt had been waiting for.

"That's why you're one of the best," he said. "You think like a true businessman."

Matt folded his arms and leaned back in his chair, trying to conjure a comeback that might segue into the topic of this new management job, but Brayton went on. "How are you feeling about this project, by the way? Things coming along as you'd hoped?"

Matt shrugged. "Better, actually. Lucky for us, the Singles Inc. in-house development team wasn't a hard act to follow. From what I understand, they're data programmers, not Web designers. Most of them are thrilled to have this taken off their plate. I guess Singles Inc. has been growing faster than anyone expected and they don't admit to having much Web-design experience or the time to deal with the site maintenance. They're busy enough with the back-end data."

Brayton snagged a wayward paper clip from the table and began tapping it against the arm of his chair. "It's always nice to work without resistance. Outsourcing isn't always so well received."

"We don't have any problems where that's concerned."

Brayton looked up at the screen. "I think Andy will like what you've done so far. Not only is the image updated, you've made quite a few good improvements to the design."

"The drop-out rate was one of the first things we looked at," Matt explained. "Far too many people were starting the survey, then not finishing." He flipped back to one screen in particular. "At the beginning of the registration process we've got information letting people know how long to expect the survey to take." Advancing forward, he added, "Then we've got the option on every screen to save the answers and come back another time. We think people don't realize how comprehensive it is, get halfway through and quit out of the program, not coming back because they don't want to do the work all over again. With the new design they not only know what to expect from the outset, but if they run out of time, they don't have to redo the questions they already answered."

"That's a great idea. Completely obvious but apparently overlooked in the original design."

Those had been Carly's ideas, as well. He hadn't expected they'd complement each other so well on the job, never having worked on a project with her before. Where he had the eye for art and design and was good at the bells and whistles, Carly focused on human behavior, asking herself who were the users, what did they want, where would they go and what turned them on and off. She had a knack for bringing up all kinds of angles he hadn't thought of, points that seemed so basic but had completely missed his radar.

A side of him wanted to bring her back to review some of the projects he'd recently worked on just to see what she'd come up with.

If only she'd talk to him.

"And how are things with you and Carly?" Brayton asked. "Everything all right there?"

Matt swallowed and put on a good face. "It's going fine," he murmured, hoping his smile helped sell the statement.

"I know Andy and I have been giving you two a little riling over those survey results."

A little? They'd been making such a deal out of it Matt had expected a minister to walk through the door any minute and marry them on Brayton's command.

"No one expects you to fall in love," Hall went on. "But I did find it ironic that Carly ended up matching your survey closer than anyone." He grinned. "It proves my instincts."

Matt grinned even though he had no idea where Hall was going with this.

Brayton stopped tapping the paper clip and instead began snapping it under his thumbnail. "If you recall, I hired you with the intent of pairing you two up someday. I always had that feeling you would be dynamite as a team."

They were explosive all right.

"Which is why I'm somewhat concerned about the tension between you two."

"Tension?" The word came out two octaves too high.

Brayton shrugged. "I could be wrong. I'm just sensing you

might be having trouble working as a team. That could be my fault. I haven't exactly pushed either of you to do much consulting on your projects. You both do a pretty good job on your own. Maybe it's hard having to suddenly share the decision-making process instead of running with your own ideas."

Matt narrowed his eyes. "Has someone expressed concerns?"

"Only my observations, though I don't have any complaints about this project so far."

Clearing the nerves from his throat, Matt sat up in his chair and responded with assurance. "Carly and I are getting along fine. Sure, maybe it's awkward having to run things by someone other than the client, but I think we're weathering the bumps and will do a superb job for the company."

"Yes, and I've got ideas for expansion and I can't carry out those ideas if my best designers can't play well in the sandbox with each other."

This was the exact segue Matt had been waiting for in his quest to bring up this rumored design team and their need for a new manager. Unfortunately, he was feeling as though he was being scolded, and bucking for a promotion right now suddenly seemed like a bad idea. Obviously, Brayton had concerns that Matt needed to resolve.

"I assure you, Carly and I are fine. She's a brilliant designer with some fantastic insights. In fact, I'm finding our strengths support each other in ways I hadn't expected. I doubt even after this project is through I'll design another Web site without getting her take on it—and I'd like to think she'll come away from this project feeling similarly. If you're sensing tension, it's probably the intensity we're bringing to the table, wanting to make sure this project goes off without a hitch."

He took a breath and hoped his assurances had worked.

Everything he'd said was true. He had begun to uncover a newfound respect for Carly. All he had to do now was get Brayton to focus on the project they were doing instead of this little rift that had come between them, at least until he made one more concerted effort to square things away with her. It appeared now that his future depended on it.

Brayton tossed the paper clip back on the table and rose from his chair. "That seems fair enough." Nodding toward the monitor, he added, "You're definitely doing a good job here. Keep it up."

Then he walked out the door, leaving Matt feeling as though he'd just dodged a bullet. He had no idea any of his problems with Carly had made their way to Brayton's office. Apparently, the walls at Hall Technologies were thinner than he'd expected. He'd hoped time would loosen the strain between them, but it now looked as if he didn't have much. Glancing at his watch, he speculated if he should try to get her to open up before they gave their presentation. Surely, if she knew Hall was expressing concerns, they could at least agree to put up a front for the sake of their careers.

He had almost a half hour before the meeting. Would that be enough time? Pushing away from the table, he decided to give it a shot.

10

CARLY AND BEV stepped into Lone Dog, one of the last independent coffee shops in the area that hadn't been taken over by the big chains. It was busy this time of day between the tail end of the lunch rush and those dropping in for an early-afternoon coffee, and after ordering two double lattes, the women tucked themselves next to a partition while they waited for their order.

"So, big meeting with Singles Inc. today?" Bev asked.

Carly nodded. "We're running our mock-ups by their marketing director to see if he likes the direction we're going in." She checked her watch. "In fact, I hope these coffees don't take too long. The meeting's in twenty minutes, and I should try to get there early to see if Matt needs any last-minute help."

Bev scoffed. "Matt needing help? Would he admit to it if he did?"

"Probably not, though I have to say he's been more cooperative than I'd expected. I thought I'd have to fight tooth and nail to get him to accept my ideas, but—*shock*—he's actually liked some of them."

"Why wouldn't he? You've got good ideas."

"I guess I always thought Matt wouldn't like any idea that wasn't his, good or bad. That's the way guys like him usually are." Although Carly had to admit this wasn't the first time Matt had thrown a wrench in her definition of *guys like him*.

Though she'd always seen him as cocky and flippant, more than once since they'd landed on this project together he'd surprised her with a gesture that came off very warm and considerate, as if inside that arrogant exterior a kind and thoughtful man existed.

Still, her smarter side warned her not to let her guard down, remembering that Matt Jacobs served only Matt Jacobs and she'd best keep that in mind lest she turn a blind eye and end up burned.

"I think you're too hard on him. Sure, he's not the warm, fuzzy type and he hasn't gone out of his way to mingle with the crew, but you haven't cut the guy a break since he knocked you off that first project." Then Bev smiled. "Except for your detour in the lab, of course."

Carly took a deep breath and sighed. "I suppose I should try harder to get along."

"That or get him back in the lab." Bev winked.

Carly opened her mouth to tell Bev to drop her ideas about she and Matt ever having sex again when a comment from the other side of the partition caught her attention.

"You should see the crack security around Singles Inc. It took me all of four minutes to break into the survey data, and most of that involved figuring out how they'd separated our survey results from their mainstream population."

It was Brian Shanahan, and Bev and Carly shared a silent glance wondering what the man was talking about—and, more importantly, to whom.

"So you've really got everyone's answers?"

It was a woman's voice. Carly suspected it was Suzie Novak, one of the summer interns they'd just hired.

Though Brian lowered his voice, they both heard him reply,

"Sure, how do you think Matt and Carly ended up with the project? By chance?"

Their jaws dropped, and without waiting for another word, Carly stepped around the low wall to find Brian and Suzie sharing a late lunch, Brian nearly choking on his focaccia sandwich when he caught the look in Carly's eyes.

She put on a smile for the intern but stared at Brian in a way that would frighten small children and most adults. "May I have a word with you?"

Brian swallowed his mouthful of sandwich. "Carly, I was just telling Suzie here—"

"Outside," she ordered, pointing toward the door.

He didn't miss the insistence in her tone. Setting down his sandwich, he excused himself while the two women escorted him out the door and down the sidewalk, away from the café tables and lingering crowd.

"Are you out of your mind?" Carly asked.

"That wasn't how it sounded," insisted Brian.

Bev folded her arms across her chest. "It sounded to me like you were on the verge of blabbing about Carly cheating on the survey." She eyed Carly. "I told you he had loose lips."

"What's the big deal?" Brian asked. "The survey's over and done with. Nobody cares how you two got assigned anymore."

"Oh, Mr. Hall would care all right," Carly scolded. "And Matt! Do you have any idea what Matt would do if he knew?"

Brian's caged look left Carly with a sick feeling in her stomach.

"You didn't."

"No, I didn't. He'd heard it somewhere else before he said anything to me about it." Pointing a finger, he defended, "I assumed one of you told him."

Her sickness welled. *"Matt knows?"* She placed her fingers to her temples to keep her head from exploding. "I can't believe this. He'll go straight to Hall."

Brian shrugged. "He hasn't yet. If he was going to run to Hall, he'd have done it ages ago."

Carly's ache halted, replaced by something more dire. "What do you mean *ages ago?*"

"Since he found out about the survey. He said he'd keep it to himself and he obviously has. I think you're overreacting."

Carly stood and stared, trying to sort through the information.

"You're telling me Matt's known about this for a while?"

"Yeah, I guess. It was just a couple days after the results were announced. It's like I said, if he was going to do something about it, he would have by now. It's old news. You shouldn't sweat it."

Carly's eyes met Bev's, the look on her face confirming every angry thought beginning to pool and boil.

"He knew days after the results," Bev said, as if Carly hadn't heard it or might have missed the significance of that fact. But she hadn't missed a thing. She knew exactly what that meant. It meant Matt had known they weren't the least bit compatible when he'd seduced her in the project room. He'd known the whole thing was a farce when he'd whispered those suggestions in her ear, the idea that they were perfect for each other, that they should explore this thing between them, that they should rip their clothes off and see exactly how compatible they were.

"Brian, I'm serious. Are you sure he knows we fudged the results?"

"He came up and asked me about it. I thought one of you had told him."

"When exactly was that?"

"Practically the day after they announced the results. Like, that following Monday. See? He's known all along and you've been fine." Brian quickly darted back inside the Lone Dog.

Fine?

She clenched her teeth as her throat closed up in a mixture of anger and humiliation. He'd known. He'd known all along. And instead of confronting her with the truth or turning her in to the boss, he'd used the information to get her out of her skirt, to take advantage of her in the most intimate way possible.

The thought made her dizzy—or maybe it was because she'd begun to hyperventilate. "I can't believe this," she said. "I can*not* believe this."

Closing her eyes and swallowing back tears, she wondered how she could be so naive. How could she have allowed herself to be used by him? A hot rush of embarrassment swept through her. She'd stood naked in front of him, offered herself to him after he'd gone on about the chemistry between them. How could she be so stupid? She'd seen his answers to the survey. She knew he was a self-serving, egomaniacal jerk. How could she have forgotten and gone along with him so willingly? She should have suspected something.

"Carly," Bev said, placing a hand on her shoulder and looking concerned. "You're pale as a ghost. Are you okay?"

Carly shot out a mock laugh. "I'm ten miles from okay. The only question now is, how quickly can I kill him?"

"Okay, Carly, we need to think about this first," Bev warned, but fury had already taken over Carly.

"There's nothing to think about. Matt Jacobs is a scumbag and it's about time everyone knew it."

"Don't do anything rash. Let's go back in, get our coffees and talk about this."

"I lost my taste for coffee," she said, then turned toward the curb and began storming across the street. She heard Bev make one last pitch, but she was beyond logic and reason at that moment. All she cared about was dealing with this—*all of this*—right now, because the more she considered what she had to be angry over, the longer the list became.

Starting with Brayton Hall and his foolish idea for the survey. If he'd just assigned the project to her as she'd deserved—*as he'd done for Matt*—she wouldn't have had to cheat her way on it in the first place. In fact, she didn't even consider what she'd done as cheating. She'd simply made restitution, righted a wrong, and she refused to look at it any other way.

Stepping off the curb, she darted around a large stone planter filled with marigolds to avoid colliding with a group of workers from AutoTronics, a large component manufacturer that leased the building next to hers. She chose the detour over slowing down and nodding pleasantries, and as she rounded the corner at the Happy Lantern, another rush of tears threatened to spoil her anger.

She couldn't believe that she'd actually fought a crush over the man. Too many times over the last week she'd reflected on their lovemaking, wondering how she might be able to go back for seconds without getting her heart broken. He'd apologized for the things he'd said, and on more than one occasion she'd nearly apologized, too, her need for a second taste strong enough to make her compromise her ultimate needs.

Thank God she hadn't. The only thing worse than being manipulated by a shallow snake like Matt Jacobs would have been actually groveling to the man, offering a truce in the hope of getting him in the sack again.

Just the thought angered her more, and as she pushed through the glass doors of Hall Technologies, she swallowed back the vise on her throat, took her anger and used it to feed her ire.

Passing her desk, as well as Matt's, she headed straight for the conference room, where she found him sitting at the table, alone.

"How dare you!" she cried, slamming her hands down on the table in front of him.

His eyes widened in shock. "What?"

"Let's explore this compatibility of ours? I think we might be *perfect* for each other?"

He looked confused but backed from the table anyway, shaking his head and shrugging as his only response.

She leaned in to take up the slack. "You knew about the survey. You knew my answers were bogus when you seduced me in the lab."

The confusion drained from his face.

"Oh, yes. I found out about that," she said.

He held up two hands as if she were holding a gun to his chest. "Look, Carly," he started. "I don't know what you're thinking—"

"I'm thinking you're a low-down, dirty degenerate who took advantage of the information you had to get me out of my panties."

Looking him in the eye and saying it out loud brought that clench back to her throat. The one that usually preceded a flood of tears. But she willed them away, wanting to make certain he didn't see an ounce of the hurt and disappointment vying inside her.

"Now wait a minute—"

"No, you wait. As of this instant, I'm off this project. And if Mr. Hall wants to know why, I'm highly tempted to blurt out the whole story." Matt's eyes filled with fear and Carly couldn't hold back her laugh. "Oh, yes. You think I won't hang myself over what I did? You're wrong. I'll accept every consequence that's coming to me before I spend another second working next to you."

He flicked his eyes to the door, then looked back at her. "Don't be rash. We need to talk this over. Later. When you can be calm."

"Calm? You want me to be *calm?* You tricked me into having sex with you!"

He eyed the open door once more, then had the nerve to shush her. "Carly, you seriously need to keep your voice down."

"And you seriously need to get a clue that I'm pretty pissed off right now and don't give a squat who knows about it or who finds out why."

He lowered his voice. "We could both get in trouble here. You aren't exactly innocent yourself, you know."

She gasped. "I think tricking a coworker into taking her clothes off is a little more serious than faking a few answers on a survey. And you know what?" she asked, leaning so far over the table she nearly lost her footing. "If they fire me, I don't care! At least that means I won't have to look at your slimy face ever again."

"I didn't trick you."

"You knew about the survey before I walked into that lab."

"Yes, but I had every intention of telling you what I knew."

She choked on a laugh. "Really? Before or after you had your hands up my skirt?"

"What the hell is going on in here!"

Carly spun around to find Mr. Hall standing in the doorway, his expression not nearly as amused as Andy McGee's, who was standing squarely behind him.

Matt shot to his feet. "There's been a little misunderstanding between Carly and me. If we could have a few moments alone, I'm sure we could square things away."

"I wouldn't come within ten feet of you again, much less ever get caught alone," Carly spat. "Go ahead and tell them why," she threw in.

"If you'll just—" Matt said, but Mr. Hall cut him off.

"Enough," he said, his mouth pressed into a firm line. "Andy, I think we'll need to reschedule this meeting. Carly, take the afternoon off and go calm yourself down. And you," he said, pointing a firm finger at Matt, "I want to see you in my office immediately."

Matt looked as though he'd just been sucker punched, and though Carly was almost certain she was soon to be fired, she felt a slight flutter of glee over the thought that at least Matt might end up out the door with her.

"Me?"

"Now, Jacobs."

Clearly it was Matt's turn to show a little rage, and Carly stood entirely smug as she watched him gather his papers and storm out the door, daggers shooting from his eyes as he gave her one last glance.

But as the three men filtered out the doorway, leaving her in the quiet of the aftermath, a deep breath brought with it a question she hadn't stopped to consider.

What exactly had she just done?

11

"I'M NOT GOING TO ask what that was all about," Brayton Hall said from behind his sleek glass-top desk. "The only salvation is that Andy McGee has found this entertaining. I'm not nearly as amused."

Brayton's face had taken on the exact shade of pink to match his shirt, and Matt feared what that meant. He'd never seen Hall angry before. Usually jovial bordering on goofy, the worst Matt had ever witnessed was a serious tone in the man's voice. This red-faced look of disgust was entirely new, and Matt wished like hell it wasn't being directed at him.

"I'm sorry, I don't know what—" he attempted.

"Let me bottom-line this for you, Matt. I pride myself in finding jewels in this industry and I happen to think you're one of them. You've got the talent, creativity and salesmanship to do better than most." He picked up a pen and began clicking the top. *Click* open. *Click* closed. *Click* open. *Click* closed. Hall rarely held a conversation of any length without fiddling with something, and at this particular moment Matt didn't need the distraction.

"I'm sure you've heard the rumors about this new design team I've been considering," Brayton added.

Matt nodded.

"You're my first choice to head it up. I need someone with charisma who can think outside the box and get clients excited about the job we'll do for them, and you've got that in the bag."

Okay, this was good, and Matt might have allowed his mood to brighten if Brayton's expression wasn't hinting that a big *but* was coming up.

"The only problem is I need a team environment with a leader who can inspire and motivate staff."

There it was. The big but.

"I assure you I can do that," Matt replied. "This thing with Carly—"

"Funny thing about Carly," Brayton interrupted. "She's my toss-up. When it comes to everything you're lacking, she's spot-on, but she's more traditional in her thinking and she doesn't wow the clients the way you do. She's my best candidate when it comes to team dynamics, but she won't give clients the cutting edge they're looking for." He clicked the pen faster. "So here's the rub. Do I pick what's best for the client or what's best for the staff?"

"I can be both."

"It's what I'd been banking on, but I'm not seeing it." Matt opened his mouth to argue, but Hall's clicking pen kept grating on his nerves. It beat in his head. And just as his annoyance with the thing brimmed, Hall tossed it on the desk with a clink, leaned back in his chair and crossed an ankle over his knee.

"Let me tell you about this survey," Hall said. "It wasn't set up to impress Singles Inc., like everyone thinks. I'd already had their business before I came up with the idea, just like I'd already picked you for the job. The whole point of the survey

nothing at all. This time he'd hit the wall while there was still another chance to scale it, and knowing how shitty life was with no options, he couldn't consider turning back.

So he rose from his chair, intent to make this work, though he had no idea how. He'd be lucky if Carly even talked to him, much less put on a happy face for work Monday morning. And given he was batting a thousand when it came to making things worse instead of better, he wasn't holding on to a lot of confidence.

But he had to give it a try, so as he walked to the door he contemplated the best way to get through to Carly in the hopes of making amends.

And as if Brayton had seen the dilemma on his face, he called out just as Matt stepped out of the room, "You might consider giving honesty a shot."

THIRTY MINUTES later Matt stood in front of a quaint bungalow in northern Marin that looked as if it had been pulled from the pages of a little girl's coloring book. Painted bright pink with white trim, it stood like a child's playhouse in the middle of an oversize lot. A pathway lined with red and white rose bushes led up to a bright yellow door, an odd color considering the pulled-taffy look of the rest of the house. Then again, nothing in this picture seemed quite right. The driveway housed a silver Pontiac Grand Prix way too sporty and contemporary for the scene. He would have expected Cinderella's pumpkin carriage instead or maybe a pink VW Bug with a weathered white silk flower attached to the antenna.

He checked the address in his hand and wondered if Hall had written the number down wrong, but the street name was clear and this was a small court of only a half dozen houses.

He supposed if he got the number wrong, the Disney character that lived here would probably know which house was really Carly's. So, taking a breath, he headed up the path and rapped on the door.

Footsteps on the other side were swift and sharp, and when the door flung open, he didn't expect to see Carly actually standing there. *This is really her house?*

The look on her face mirrored his.

He opened his mouth to speak, but she stiffened her lip and slammed the door in his face before he could offer a greeting. Dammit. He wasn't in the mood for any more games. He'd just had to take it in the backside from Hall and had valiantly kept his mouth shut about Carly and the survey. She owed him five minutes of her time.

Pounding on the door with more vigor, he called out, "Carly, open up. We need to talk."

The door swung back open. "Who told you where I live?"

"Hall gave me your address."

"Good. Then after he fires me I can sue him for breach of privacy."

She moved to slam the door a second time, but he jammed his foot in the threshold and braced it with his hand. "I'm serious. We need to talk this through."

"There's nothing to talk about. Thanks to you, I've probably lost my job. I think we've done enough talking for one lifetime, and if you think—"

"If anyone's losing their job, it's me, not you."

That shut her up. She clearly hadn't expected to hear that, and in response she jutted her chin and said, "Good," but the sentiment didn't quite reach her eyes.

He bit down his anger in the hope of appealing to that

little soft spot she was trying to hide. "Please, Carly, I need your help."

She stiffened her spine. "Why should I help you?"

"Because half of this is your fault."

She scoffed, and Matt used her momentary shock to push his way through the door and into…the strangest-looking pink oasis he'd ever seen. Three steps to the right was a pink kitchen remodeled circa 1985. To the left was a dining room with no table. Looking down, he found himself standing on a path of rose-colored tiles. Did marble come in that shade naturally?

"I didn't invite you in."

"I didn't ask for an invite."

He heard the door slam behind him and her footsteps at his back.

"I can't believe you've got the gall to show your face here after what you did."

Now, there was another thing he was officially tired of hearing today. Turning on his heels, he folded his arms across his chest. "Tell me again what it is I did?"

"You conned me into having sex with you, for starters."

"I didn't con you into anything. I made a few seductive comments and you took the ball and ran with it."

She clasped her hands to her hips. "You knew we weren't the least bit compatible when you seduced me in the lab."

"And so did you."

She opened her mouth for a comeback, but nothing came out. Yes, there it was. The slight technicality she'd like to conveniently ignore.

"You knew as much as I did your answers were phony, but you were happy to go along anyway. Hell, I'd barely made the suggestion before you were tonguing my thumb and climbing up my lap."

She gasped as if she'd just been slapped, yet she was still at a loss for words. What could she say? She knew he had her by the horns.

Closing the distance between them, he took her slack jaw in his hand. "Play the sweet prude at the office, but spare it on me. I'm well familiar with the hot-blooded sex kitten you've buttoned up under that collar."

She snapped her mouth shut and jerked her chin from his hand, but the tip of her nose had turned red, telling him he'd scored a direct hit.

With slightly less conviction than she'd had a moment ago, she retreated a step and asked, "What do you want from me?"

"I want to clear the air between us so we can go back to work Monday happy as clams."

"You're off to a heck of a start."

"I'm laying it all on the table, your crap, as well as mine." He stepped in to make up the distance between them. "My job is on the line, and that's too important to me to ride it all on a simple apology. I could come in here, grovel at your feet and hope you'll lose the chip on your shoulder, but I've got too much at stake to leave this in your hands." He pointed a finger to her chest. "Here and now, you and I are going to air two years of animosity between us, and I'm not leaving until every last morsel has been thrown on the table."

She pressed her lips into a slit. "You're going to have a long wait if you think you can pin your problems on me."

"Trust me, I've got plenty to apologize for. I know I stepped in and walked all over your realm when you'd been sold another story by Hall. And in the two years since, I never went out of my way to make things better between us. I made the fool's mistake in thinking I didn't need you or anyone else at the firm to get ahead, and you'll be happy to know that's come back to bite me in the ass. I have a talent for putting my foot in my mouth when it comes to you and I won't even begin to individually list and tabulate every ill-formed comment where that's concerned."

Then he stepped close and pinned her against her entryway wall. "But the one thing I won't cop to is this nonsense about taking advantage of you. And I'm sure as hell not going to apologize for making love to you."

Her eyes turned to wide blue saucers. The little blush at the tip of her nose spread across her cheeks. She parted those stiff lips and sucked in a breath when he dipped his chin to look her in the eye.

Lowering his voice, he added, "Call me a lot of things, Carly, but I don't take advantage of women. Say I've made some underhanded moves, but don't tell me I had to trick you into having sex with me. If you want the real story, I'd only been teasing you, with every intention of coming clean about the survey. But I underestimated how damned sexy you are and your ability to drive me three shades of stupid." He bent closer until his chest almost grazed her breast, and a heavy gulp slid down her throat. Her eyes dipped to his mouth and stayed there, fixated on every word as if she had to watch, as well as hear what he was saying.

The air became humid in the small space. The light from the adjoining rooms seemed to fade. And when he softened his tone, his voice played like a song between them.

"You went willingly into my arms and you know it as well as I do," he said. "And please don't tell me you regret what we shared because that was the best sex I can remember and I'd do it all over again if you'd only let me."

Pressing herself against the wall, she swept her tongue across her bottom lip, then slowly raised her eyes to his, and when their gazes met, he saw the depth of her surprise. She clearly hadn't expected a word of this, and he had to take pause and wonder just how high a tower he'd managed to build around himself.

Had she really seen none of this coming?

Shaking his head, he asked, "Did you think you were just some notch on my bedpost?"

She lightly shrugged. "I…I don't… Maybe."

He backed up a step and brushed a hand over his face. "You underestimate yourself, Carly. You're light-years from a notch on a bedpost." Taking another step away, he added, "You're the kind of woman guys fall for."

He could see he'd thrown her for a loop. Gone was the defiant stiff chin and pursed angry brow, and in their place was a woman who'd just been plunked upside the head by his admission. And he wasn't sure if that was good or bad.

"What do you want from me?" she asked again, her voice soft and hesitant.

"Honesty. I want to know what I can do to cure this tension between us. I want to know how we can find a truce and keep it." Feeling a sudden need for air, he stepped into a living area that, while sparsely furnished, was thankfully devoid of all things pink. Opting for an upholstered blue-and-white-striped chair, he moved through the room and plopped down.

"I wasn't kidding about my job, Carly. Hall's pissed—and he's pissed at me."

"I'm sure he's pissed at me, too," she said. She hadn't

moved from the hallway and was only now taking gradual steps into the room. "I was the one who cheated on the survey."

"Yeah, well, he doesn't know about that."

"You didn't tell him?"

The level of shock in her voice brought a sour taste to his mouth. She didn't have to be so stunned that he hadn't blown the whistle on her, though he shouldn't have expected more. She'd had a bad impression of him from the start, and in her defense, he'd never made the slightest effort to correct it.

"No, I didn't tell him," he said, trying to reassure her. "That's your business, not mine, and it wouldn't have mattered to Hall anyway. In his eyes, you get along with everyone and I don't. If you have a problem, it's only because you're dealing with me."

"He said that?"

"He might as well have."

She fell silent for a long time before she quietly admitted, "That's not fair."

"He's probably more spot-on than I'd care to confess." After all, it was Hall who'd told him to give honesty a shot. And—lo and behold—it seemed to work. Matt was sitting here in Carly's living room, and not only hadn't she called the police, she wasn't even yelling at him anymore. Cupping his face in his hands, he rubbed his eyes and considered his situation. At this point he had no problem laying his soul on the line if it would fix things here. The only question was, could Carly be honest with him?

She spoke up then. "I'm sorry I blew up at the office and got you in trouble. Monday morning, I plan to straighten that out with Mr. Hall and—"

He looked up from his hands. "You aren't apologizing to Hall for any of this."

She slipped into the chair opposite his. "Storming into the conference room in a conniption fit is most definitely something I need to apologize for. And I don't care what Mr. Hall thinks, you don't deserve to take the blame for it all. If anything, he's the one who should be apologizing for dreaming up this stupid survey in the first place." That angry stiffness returned to her chin. "I shouldn't have had to fix a survey to get a spot on that project. I should have been given it based on the work I've done for him all these years."

"Carly, he didn't put you on the project because he already knows your capabilities. I'm the one being tested here, not you. It's the reason I'm on the hook for how things have turned out. He already knows he can pair you with anyone and the job will run smoothly. I'm another story."

She pursed her brow. "What do you mean you're being tested? Tested for what?"

Did she not know about the new design team or the open management position? He thought everyone had heard that rumor.

For a brief moment he considered holding back, not knowing how she'd react to finding out they were both in line for the same job. But then he remembered Hall's comment about honesty, how so far it had been working in his favor.

"Did you know there was a management job opening up?" he asked.

The quick change in her expression said she did. "I heard a rumor," she muttered. "I don't know how much truth—"

"It's true. Hall confirmed it for me this afternoon." The dark turn to her eyes left him fearing he'd just obliterated all the progress they'd made, but he had to come clean. "You and I are both candidates for the job."

Her eyes widened. "Me?"

"I told you, Carly—you don't have anything to prove when it comes to Hall. He's already confident in your abilities, but he admitted he's torn between the two of us. He feels I'm better with the clients and you're better with the staff, and unless one of us proves the ability to do both, who knows which way he'll go."

For the longest time she simply sat and stared, those violet-blue eyes reflecting his same feelings about the dilemma they faced.

"So we're competing for the same job, yet he expects us to get along and function as a team," she finally said.

He nodded.

"And he assumes we can because the survey said we were perfect for each other."

"Yes."

She frowned. "Remind me again why you didn't tell him I fixed the survey? It sounds to me like it would have resolved all of this and landed you that management spot."

He had to admit he'd asked himself that same question more than a dozen times on his way to her house, but no matter how he turned it over, the result stayed the same. "I'm not a perfect man, Carly, but I won't stoop to making myself look good by making you look bad."

A pained look crossed her face before she pushed up from the chair and stormed out of the room.

"Carly?" he asked as he heard her footsteps round the hall into the kitchen. Cupboard doors slammed, drawers rolled open and closed while those sharp steps echoed through the room. "We need to talk about this." He began to rise from the chair, but before he could, she came back with two bottles of red wine and a pair of tumblers.

"I don't drink much," she said. "This was left over from a party. It's the only alcohol I have." Handing him a corkscrew, she dropped one of the bottles in his lap. "This is probably a bad idea, but I could really go for a drink right now."

He stared at the bottle in his hand. "You're right," he said. "This is a bad idea." Then he peeled back the lead cap and twisted the corkscrew into the top. "But it's the best bad idea I've heard in a long time."

12

"Mr. Hall is a big dumb jerk!"

Matt glanced at the angry pout on Carly's face and realized she was right: she didn't drink much. He'd only now refilled her glass of wine—and not a large one at that—and already she was demonstrating the effects of the first.

"You already said that three times," he replied, fighting back a chuckle.

Somehow the two of them had ended up stretched out on the fuzzy shag rug that covered the hard oak floor of her living room. At Matt's side was a half-empty bottle of wine and a fireplace filled with a dozen lit candles. Short of the cat that had taken up residence on his butt and a meager glass of wine that had gone straight to Carly's head, the scene might have actually been romantic.

Carly was lying on her back, staring at the ceiling, a blue-and-white-striped seat cushion acting as her pillow. "I'll say it three more times before the night is out." She lifted her head to take a sip of her wine. "I'm really mad at him. He should not be putting us in this position."

She set the wine back on the coffee table at her head, plopped against the cushion and huffed.

"We've been through this. We agreed we'd help each other

out, do the best job we could and let Hall decide in the end who he wants to manage the new unit."

They'd come to the decision after feeling each other out and realizing neither of them was willing to step aside and let the other have the job. Apparently, Carly had her eyes zeroed in on that promotion as much as he did, and the only truce they could find was making an honest effort to help one another strengthen their weaknesses and let the best man—or woman—win.

And, ironically, once they'd made that decision, their differences had melted away like ice cream on hot asphalt. It seemed once they'd been honest with each other about what they wanted, all the stress had eased between them and they were able to relax.

"I still think he could have saved everyone a ton of trouble by just giving it to us straight from the start."

"Well, Hall's never been one to take the standard route with anything."

She lifted her head and eyed him with all seriousness. "He doesn't, does he?"

"No, but we've talked enough about Hall today. We were playing Truth or Truth, and you never answered your question."

The game started out as a twist on the classic Truth or Dare, Matt deciding the option of having a dare was probably a bad idea, but both of them wanting to end the day having aired every grievance between them. Thus the game Carly coined Truth or Truth.

"I forget my question," she said.

Propped on his elbows and lying on his stomach, he pointed his thumb toward his backside. "What's up with your cat?"

Carly sat up and gasped. "Mr. Doodles! Get off Matt!" She swatted at the cat, but the gray tabby didn't budge. "Gawd, he's such a bad cat. He doesn't listen to anything I say."

"He's not that bad. I only wondered if he had a fetish for men's butts is all."

"No, he's just not well trained. Honestly, I grew up in apartments, and this is the first time I've ever had an animal. I don't know what I'm doing with him. And there's no such thing as a cat trainer. Trust me—I looked."

"You've never lived in a house before?"

She leaned against the cushion and stared proudly at the space. "This is my first and it's all mine. I bought it myself, you know. I wanted to make sure my kids grew up in a real house with a real yard."

"And a badly trained cat."

"Exactly!" she laughed.

He watched as she stared at the ceiling and envisioned her dream, her face filled with such hope and pride it felt contagious.

"Your parents could never afford a home?" he asked, taking a casual sip of his wine.

She snorted. "My dad could probably afford three homes. It's just that all those mistresses get expensive." She furrowed her brow. "It wouldn't surprise me if he did own homes in a couple states. For as little as we see him, he's probably one of those guys with a bunch of families none of us know about."

Matt gaped. "Are you serious?"

She shrugged. "I really don't know. I get so frustrated with my mother. Every time I try to pump her for information she gets upset and we end up fighting." She turned and placed a hand over her mouth. "Oh, don't get me wrong. I love my mom. She's the only thing steady in mine and Jodi's lives and she works her fingers to the bone. I just don't understand why she hasn't dumped him for something better. I'd never let a man treat me like that." Then her expression soured. "It hurts the whole family, not just her."

Matt hadn't meant to open sore wounds, and judging by the bitter pain in her eyes, it seemed her father stung sharp and deep.

Another thing the two of them had in common.

He redirected the subject, preferring that gratified look he'd seen before. "Well, now you've got a home of your own."

"In all its pink splendor." She turned her head and met his gaze with a smile. "You ever hate a color so bad you never want to see it on anything again?"

"You aren't fond of pink?"

"Nobody can handle this much. You should have seen it before I ripped out the carpet."

He scanned the room. "I can imagine."

"It's the only reason I got the place at the price I paid. Nobody could handle all the pink, not even the flippers. I bought it way under market, and now it's just a matter of time and money before I turn it into the home I want."

Matt looked around and took it all in, his reaction a mix of pride and pity. On one hand, he admired her for being so resourceful in chasing after her dreams. On the other, this quirky oversize dollhouse was a pathetic start that would take a lot more than paint and elbow grease to bring it around. Through a sliding glass door he saw a backyard of little more than mown weeds. Though the wood floors weren't pink, they were long overdue for a good sanding and polish. Kitchens and baths were expensive to rip out, and even once landscaped, this oversize lot would be big enough to require plenty of constant care.

Rather than a savvy investment, the house looked like a little girl's desperate attempt to create the home she'd been denied, and his heart went out to her. The need in her eyes made him want this for her as much as she did, and as a man who hadn't grown up with a real home, either, he understood the desire.

"Hey, wasn't that more like three questions?" she asked.

He smiled. "I guess it's your turn."

She studied him for a while, the smile slowly fading from her lips and sobering her playful expression.

"So...what happened with the Nationals?" she said. "If you don't mind me asking."

Though his failed career in baseball wasn't his favorite topic, he shrugged and shook his head, well accustomed to dealing with questions. A guy didn't leave town with a bright future ahead of him and return with nothing without people wanting to hear the story.

He took a quick sip of his wine and smacked his lips. "I wasn't good enough. It's as simple as that. I had the national talent, but not the work ethic to make something of it. I'd been cocky and immature, assuming I was better than I was. And though a dozen coaches and trainers had tried to warn me, I never gave it my best before it was too late. They released me before I got it through my head that hard work was just as important as natural talent. And in a tough field like baseball, you needed both to be successful."

"I'm sorry." Her voice was somber and that annoyed him. He'd spent enough of his life feeling sorry for himself, wallowing in grief and anger over that devastating blow, and like an alcoholic being offered a drink, he didn't like people pulling him back to that state again, even unintentionally.

"Don't be," he said. "We don't always get what we want out of life. It's how we handle what's left that matters."

It was the line Stu had given him and it had become the rule he lived by. It was only when he'd really listened to those words and accepted their meaning that he'd started to turn his life around. He'd gone back to school to study graphic arts and discovered in the process he had more talents than just baseball. Stu called it a great gift to be able to remake a life once failed, and Matt was determined not to let this one slip through his fingers.

"And you took what was left and became a successful Web designer," she said.

"I'm trying."

Her voice softened and she rested a comforting hand on his arm. "There's no trying about it. You really are very good, you know. I'm not just saying that." She pulled a reluctant smile to her lips. "I'd give anything for your eye for art. I've tried to mimic some of the things you've done before, but it never comes out right. You've got a gift that just can't be taught."

There was something in the way she said it, not only sincerity but respect, that made the compliment mean more to him than he would have expected. He felt her words deep in his chest. In a place he reserved for very few. And it occurred to him at that moment how much her opinion mattered to him.

Weeks ago—heck, even hours ago—he would have scoffed at the idea that Carly's opinion mattered. Maybe it was that she'd never complimented him before. Maybe her persistent disdain for him had always kept him in armor. But here, with their shields down and their hearts slightly ajar, he realized how much her approval really meant to him.

Staring in those bright blue eyes, the end result of two years of anger showed its face to him and he finally saw it for what it had been. He'd treated Carly badly out of jealousy. Not jealousy on the job but jealousy of the fact that this woman everyone loved wouldn't turn her affections toward him. She was the ray of sunshine beaming on everyone she passed but clouding over in his presence, and he didn't realize until now how much he'd desperately wanted that sunshine, too.

In Matt's life, very few people made their way into that place in his heart. It had been cemented over too many times by affections he'd been denied. His father had been the first to close over the hole instead of fill it, and despite his mother's efforts and those of a dozen teachers and coaches, no one had been able to break the barrier Jeff Jacobs had created.

Only Stu had found an opening, had crept into that space where Matt kept the few people he cared for, and through Stu Matt had learned to let more people in. There'd been college professors and some mentors along the way, the latest being Brayton Hall, who Matt sought approval from and drank in whatever respect he could earn. But he'd known all this and had accepted the risks of opening his heart.

What he hadn't realized was that in all this time Carly Abrams had mattered, too. She'd been that slice of something special he hadn't noticed until he'd squashed it, and rather than work to make amends, he'd fallen into his old familiar ways by simply shutting her out.

"I…um…I think you can be taught some basic rules when it comes to art and design," he said hoarsely, this sudden realization leaving him shaken and a little unsettled.

She shook her head and smiled. "Not the kind of talent you've got."

She was making this hard, her expression sobering as if she'd come to some sort of revelation of her own. Maybe she'd caught the look in his eyes, maybe the fleeting effects from the wine were wearing off. He didn't know for sure, but the mood was quickly shifting, and his thoughts started drifting to places they shouldn't go.

She stretched languidly next to him, a funny smile crossing her face that disappeared just before she asked, "Did you really mean what you said before? About having sex with me all over again if I'd let you?"

His cock heard the comment and responded, but the rest of him tried to shake back the reality that they needed to go to work Monday on good terms. As much as he'd love to spend his weekend in her bed, he feared unraveling all the progress they'd made this afternoon.

Unfortunately, he'd gotten used to their game of honesty, and when he opened his mouth, he heard himself say, "I meant every word."

She grinned, then rolled onto her side, propping her head in one hand and leaving the other free to toy with the hem of his dress shirt. "I have a confession of my own."

He swallowed, not certain he should hear it.

"I didn't lie on the whole survey."

Now he knew he shouldn't have heard that. Nor should he have allowed himself the peek down her blouse into the spot where two voluptuous breasts collided into mounds of cleavage a guy could sink his face into.

"That part about the sex—that whole bit about toying with Mr. Hall—it was all a lie."

He let his eyes drop down to the teal low-rise sweats she'd changed into before he'd shown up, the ones that fell just under her navel, held in place by a little drawstring he imagined pulling off with his teeth. The thought had whisked through his mind earlier, shut out by his insistence that this visit would be about clearing the air between them and doing what he had to do to get along. At the time it had included dismissing his aching need for her and keeping his thoughts platonic.

Apparently, Carly had other ideas.

"I was embarrassed that you'd seen my answers. I didn't know what you'd think of me if you knew I had a secret dream about engaging in kinky sex."

Her eyes were focused squarely on his lips, which twitched involuntarily, his body far more responsive to her words than his conscience. It, on the other hand, was still trying to keep him from losing his job.

She let go of his shirt and began trailing a finger up his arm, tracing a line along the edge of his sleeve where he'd rolled it up at the forearm.

"But then I saw *your* answers. Did you know we answered all those questions the same?"

"We did?" he asked, not recognizing the voice that croaked from his throat.

"Uh-huh."

His hard cock pressed uncomfortably against the floor, crushed by the weight of the fat cat on his butt, so he shifted to his side, dumping Mr. Doodles to the floor, where he voiced his displeasure before scampering away. It felt good to ease the pressure, though Carly wasted no time taking advantage of his new accessibility. The finger that had been trailing his arm now made its way down toward his crotch, and his erection stiffened as if to meet her halfway.

"Carly," he said, making a last-ditch effort to keep perspective on the moment, though as her finger met the top button of his jeans, he nearly forgot where he'd been heading. "If we don't start getting along at the office, we could lose our jobs," he said, pleased he'd managed to get the sentence out while he had the chance.

"I think we got along pretty well during that hour in the lab."

When her finger passed the threshold of his jeans and made contact with the bulge inside, her eyes dropped and widened, those luscious coral lips parting in the barest hint of a gasp.

Had she really not expected she'd been turning him on?

She spread her palm over his shaft and slid her hand between his legs, the pressure testing the limits of what a man can take without buckling.

Yet he still gave it one last shot.

"Seriously, Carly, we can't afford another fight." She slid her palm back up his shaft. "I can't afford to stick my foot in my mouth and piss you off again."

"Then you should probably shut up and kiss me."

Wiggling those curvy teal hips, she scooted toward him, giving his nose a whiff of sweet peaches and wine. She let her head fall against the cushion, her hair splaying around her like a halo, her eyes teasing and her lids heavy. Her shirt stretched as her breasts settled back into perfect clutchable mounds, and the hem rode up to display a silky flat stomach, hips arched and ready for him to reach in and take hold of the offering.

And the last thing he heard was a curse sliding from his lips before he wrapped an arm around her waist, pulled her against his chest and crushed his mouth to hers.

His body sighed. Waves of aching tension slid from his limbs, escaping through his breath, while coils of hungry need slipped into their wake. He groped and sucked like a starved and thirsty teen, one arm clutching her close while the other roamed and explored, and her curvy, tender body held a land-scape of possibilities so vast he couldn't decide where to start.

Slipping a hand up under her shirt, he groaned when his fingers met with naked flesh, and she responded by arching closer, shoving the fleshy soft mound into his waiting palm. Her hand fisted his shirt, using it like a leash to pull him closer while her tongue stroked and fed. She smelled of fruit, tasted like dry red wine, and when she wrapped a leg around his waist and pressed her hips to his erection, a pulse of pleasure ripped through him so sudden and striking he grunted.

Why did this woman drive him so wild? What was it about her that took the wind from his lungs and the decency from his soul? Since they'd met he had never been able to stay lukewarm around her. He either ran scorching hot or frigidly cold, the woman digging through his layers and pulling out the best and worst in him, not settling for anything in between.

And having seen his bad side, he now wanted to show her the good.

His lips left hers and kissed a path to her ear. "We need to get to your bedroom."

She held up a limp hand and spoke through a breath. "It's that way."

Looking up, he noted the hallway at the opposite end of the room, then moved to his feet, reaching out a hand to pull her up into his arms.

She heaved in a breath and grinned when he whipped her off her feet, wrapping those delicate arms around his neck and pressing her lips to his cheek.

"Promise me we'll stay friends after this," he said, though in truth he was beyond worrying about where this was all headed. He'd begun to figure out that Carly Abrams was a woman masterful at getting her way—and he was powerless against her will. So instead of fighting like a fish swimming upstream, he might as well just shift direction and enjoy wherever the current took him.

"I'm not promising you anything," she said, proving his point to a T. "But if we can't be friends, I guarantee you can be my lover."

Sinking his teeth into her neck, he muttered, "It's a deal."

13

CARLY HADN'T forgotten what she'd learned the last time she ended up in Matt's arms. The grand realization was that when it came to him, she couldn't separate heart from body, that she was incapable of enjoying the sexy stud without losing herself to the man.

She knew exactly where she would land once Matt reached her bedroom, and it wasn't just her bed. But darned if she could be near him without opting to dismiss all that and take what she could get. He was like her own personal compulsion, an impulse item she couldn't resist at the checkout even though she knew she'd end up with buyer's remorse when she balanced her account.

She'd tried not to gleam when he'd called her a hot-blooded sex kitten. She'd swallowed down that flutter when he'd said she was the best sex he could remember. And for well over an hour she'd worked hard to forget he'd said she was the kind of woman guys fall for—noting that he hadn't necessarily been speaking about himself. He'd said *guys,* as in, *those other guys,* and she knew better than to add words that hadn't been spoken.

But despite it all, the man excited her in ways she couldn't ignore. Every time he got close her body heated and swayed, her pulse flickered and her sex clenched. It was as though he came electrically wired to set her off, to put her every nerve ending on heightened alert, and the longer she spent subjected to the charge, the weaker her defenses became. As much as she wished otherwise, as much as her mind begged her to place her affections somewhere else, Matt Jacobs was the man who lit her on fire—and there wasn't a thing she could do about it.

She'd done the safe nice-guy thing before. For once in her life she wanted that thrill only Matt could give her, and if she lost her heart in the process, she'd have to accept it as the ticket price for a ride well worth it.

Reaching the edge of her bed, he placed her on the floor and wasted no time in pulling her shirt up over her head, leaving her breasts bare and exposed. The cool air raised goose bumps on her skin, but they quickly smoothed away when he bent and took one nipple in his mouth, cupping the other with his big, warm hand. She laced her fingers through his hair and drew him close, curving her spine in an attempt at drawing nearer.

Already she was wet and ready, his sexy moans vibrating through her chest and settling between her thighs. This could be over so quickly if left up to her, but she knew he was only getting started—and where he planned to take her this time, she could barely imagine.

He switched breasts, giving the other equal attention while he moved his hands to her sweats, tugging open the drawstring and letting them pool at her feet. And when he slipped a finger between her folds, he shuddered and dropped to his knees.

"Take your clothes off," she said.

He pressed his lips to her navel and began kissing a path south. "That's not advisable if you want this to last."

He kissed lower, reaching the edge of her curls before darting east and heading toward a thigh.

Her legs weakened. His hands slid around her waist, then dug into her ass, pulling her against his mouth as he trailed his tongue in one direction, then turned the other way. She cupped her hands to his head for strength, but every press of his lips left her weaker.

"Then at least let me sit," she begged.

Accepting her request, he stood and began removing his shirt, when he caught sight of them both in the mirror.

He lifted a brow. "Mirrored closet doors?"

She glanced to the foot of her bed, where one wall of her small bedroom had been encased in floor-to-ceiling mirrored closet doors. It was one of the first things she planned to get rid of once she had the money to replace them, never getting used to her own puffy face staring back at her first thing every morning.

Matt had thrown his shirt on the floor and was pulling condoms from his wallet, the calculating look on his face not settling well with her.

"Oh, no. Don't get any ideas," she warned.

He pained. "I thought you told the truth on that survey."

"Seeing myself naked isn't my idea of a turn-on," she said. Pulling his jeans and boxers down off his waist, she saw Matt's thick cock spring forward, prompting her to add, "Now, seeing *you* naked is a different story."

He scowled and turned back her buttercup eyelet bedspread, pulling out the blue-and-yellow pillows, stacking them against the maple headboard, then settling down on the bed. He leaned back against them so he faced her mirrored wall, then held out a hand.

"Come here," he said, and she obliged, moving over his lap and straddling his legs.

"No, turn around."

She looked him in those evil, smiling eyes. "Oh, no. I told you—anything but the mirror."

"Why not?"

Though Carly had never been overly self-conscious about her body, she wasn't exactly comfortable with it, either, and making love while staring at herself wasn't tops on her list of turn-ons. "I'm telling you, if you're trying to make me frigid, force me to stare at myself naked in the mirror."

"Babe," he said, grabbing her waist and turning her around so her back was to his chest. "First rule of great sex is to be comfortable in your own skin." He spread his legs and motioned her down between them. "Sit back against me."

She followed his order, though not happily. "But—"

"Trust me," he whispered in her ear.

Reluctantly she settled against him, a spray of warming afternoon sunlight spilling from the window and warming the chill from her skin. His hard chest felt good against her back, and his erection pressed promises against the base of her spine. She really wasn't sure of this, but the wonder and anticipation over what he had in mind had her going along.

"Scoot down farther," he said. "Rest your head against my shoulder." And when she did, she found herself staring square at their reflection, Matt's tanned, handsome face smiling seductively over her shoulder, his strong arms embracing her and those firm runner's legs stretched out on either side of her hips.

Feeling much more comfortable with his naked body than hers, she decided to focus on him. He began by smoothing her hair over her shoulders, his warm breath tingling over her skin and causing her to wiggle against the hard cock at her back.

"No fidgeting," he said. "I've got lots of ideas for you and I'll have to scratch half of them if you can't do this."

"Do what?"

He pressed his lips to her neck. "Accept how beautiful you are."

A hot flush came over her, but his assuring words piqued her curiosity, and she dared to take a glance. "That's good," he whispered. "Keep your eyes focused on the mirror."

He circled his fingers around her breasts. "Look how perfect these are."

"They're small."

Cupping his hands over them, he replied, "They fit perfectly, see?" before returning to the slow massage. He smoothed his hands down her stomach and around her hips. "I love these curves."

She typically referred to it as cellulite, but she kept that opinion to herself.

"A man likes to know he's making love to a woman," he said. Then he clasped his hands to her waist. "Soft yet firm. Exactly the way I like it."

The unbridled admiration in his eyes felt contagious despite her discomfort at seeing herself sprawled naked on her bed. His hands roamed over her, trailing fingers over her collarbone and up her neck while he spoke words of appreciation, telling her what he liked about every inch of her until she actually began to believe it. And just in case she didn't, he occasionally pressed his erection to her back as proof his words were true.

Slowly she began to relax against him, mesmerized by the

feel of his warm hands and the sweet whispered sensations. She'd never considered her body especially desirable, but nestled against his, the contrast of her soft curves against his hard lines, her pale skin against his tanned, rugged flesh, it began to feel sexy. He massaged the tension from her shoulders, toyed with the dark strands of her hair until her muscles fell limp and she'd grown used to the figure staring back at her.

Instead of fretting over her reflection, she basked in the hard feel of him, the salty scent of man, the warm sun streaming over their bodies. The soft stubble of his chin occasionally scraping against her neck. And when she reached the pinnacle of comfort, he moved his hands down under her thighs and gradually parted her legs, bringing her knees toward her chest and exposing her sex to the mirror.

She stiffened. "Oh, no—"

"Yes, baby," he whispered. "I want you to see how sexy you are when you come."

She shook her head and tried to pull her legs back together. "I don't think I can—"

"Shh, yes you can." Slipping his hands between her thighs, he began stroking the flesh around her slick nub, pressing his mouth to her neck and nibbling the sensitive skin just above her shoulder. "Relax and watch the woman in the mirror. If it helps, pretend it's not you. Imagine it's an erotic movie on TV."

Her body couldn't help but respond to his touch. Sensations oozing over her, she sank heavily against him, her clit pulsing and aching for more pressure, but she had yet to glance back to the mirror. It felt so good she didn't want to ruin the pleasure.

"Come on, babe. Look in the mirror. Watch me looking at you, pleasuring you."

Reluctantly she allowed herself a glimpse, catching his face first, and for a moment he held her gaze, nodding his acceptance before guiding her down with his eyes. And when she took in the sight before her, flames of pleasure licked through her.

Her cheeks were flushed, her breasts had perked tightly, her nipples hard and pointed, and when she caught the rhythm of his fingers in the mirror circling between her legs, one hand digging into her thigh, she leaned back and soaked it all in.

She had to admit, this was ridiculously sexy. Watching them both was like watching a film with Feel-O-Vision, like some virtual sex machine that pleasured through all the senses. With his fingers spreading her open, she watched her clit pulse as he circled it, moving in close, then sweeping away, coming near, then pulling away, near and away, until she squirmed against the strain.

A film of moisture glistened her skin, making her appear surreal, and as he increased the speed, her breasts heaved as she began panting for air.

"This is hot, isn't it, baby?"

All she could do was moan.

He slipped one finger inside, and her moan deepened to a groan. "How about I talk dirty to you?"

She watched her chest rise and fall as she worked to catch her breath, the pressure between her legs mounting when he slipped a second finger inside and began circling her clit faster.

"I want to come," she begged.

"Watch it happen for me." He circled closer, brushing against her nub and nearly sending her over the edge before he pulled back away.

"Look at the need in those eyes," he whispered.

Her eyes were needy.

"Look at your beautiful mouth, lips full and moist, open for me as you move closer to the edge."

She sucked in a breath as he swept back in, stroking over her clit and sending another wash of tingles shooting through her.

"Look how you're squirming against me. You're getting me harder."

Grasping handfuls of pale yellow sheets in her fists, she arched against his hand, needing more pressure, aching for the climax he continued to deny.

"You're close, aren't you?"

"Please," she whispered, and he obeyed, moving in for the final few strokes.

"I'll give it to you, but you've got to watch."

She held her eyes on the wild, pleading woman in the mirror.

"Watch yourself shatter in my arms," he said, sweeping over her clit again. "Then you can watch me as I bring you to your knees and fuck you from behind."

The bold comment shot straight through her and she came apart in his arms, her eyes squeezing shut from the tight and violent clench between her thighs, her body convulsing against him, her back rocking against his stiff cock, getting him harder, making him ready for the promise he'd just made.

And heaven help her, but she wanted to see it. The very idea of watching him thrusting into her carried her climax for another beat before the waves settled and she calmed against his chest. Her eyes were heavy and her cheeks red as cherries.

For a long moment she rested, Matt's hands toying with her breasts, lightly stroking her nipples until her breathing resumed. She raised her eyes to his.

"My turn," he said, nudging her forward, then coaxing her to her knees.

As she stared at them both in the mirror, she saw him grab a condom and sheath himself, his erection twitching as he rolled the latex over his shaft. Then he positioned himself behind her and guided her down on all fours.

She glanced in the mirror before her, liking the image she saw staring back at her. Her hair hung haphazardly around her face, dipping over one eye the way she'd seen in sexy *Cosmopolitan* shots. Bent over like this, her breasts appeared fuller and her thighs more shapely rather than plump. Her lips and cheeks were still flushed from her climax, and with a thrill that nearly startled her she realized she actually felt sexy. In fact, she felt more than sexy. She felt hot.

"Arch your back, baby," he said, slipping two fingers into her and using them to guide his cock to her entrance.

She did, and he scooted closer, widening his legs to get lower as he clutched a hand to her hip and readied himself. Then with a smooth, slow thrust, he pushed himself inside, his face relaxing with a sigh as he slid into her slick core until the base of his shaft met the soft rounds of her ass.

"You're so tight like this," he groaned, and she arched up farther, wanting to take him in more.

Already her pulse began a steady climb as his thick, heavy cock filled her. He stroked his hands over her hips and around her waist, his eyes meeting hers in the mirror as he moved and thrust behind her. The muscles along his arms, chest and abs rolled and contorted, the veins along his pecs bulging as he gripped her tighter and increased the pressure.

The man was ravishing, statuesque in this naked form, with eyes, dark and focused, savoring her body as if it were a fine piece of art. And when she was with him like this, that's how she felt. Valuable and precious, sexy and desired, her power to move him to climax not missed in the reflection in the mirror.

His expression grew more intent, his face coloring under the stubble of his beard. She wanted to see him unravel inside her, watch this tight, controlled man succumb to complete withdrawal. The anticipation throbbed against her already-swelling sex. He wrapped his hands around her and began stroking her again, a dark smile curving his lips when her eyes met his in warning. She was brimming near the edge, and as his playful look sobered, she knew he was brimming, as well.

Pushing and stroking, they upped the beat, faster and faster until her cheeks slapped against his waist and the ache of restraint burned red in his face. "Oh, babe," he cried, then he followed it up with a curse, his gaze churning toward need as the pressure built and the pace quickened.

Digging her fingers into the eyelet comforter, ripples of pleasure swept through her, slow at first, then picking up speed as he drove them both to ecstasy. And when he pressed his lips together and the first signs of climax crossed his features, she came apart completely.

She didn't recognize the deep wail as the sound of her own voice, her tight muscles clamping hard around him as the orgasm swept her away. Her eyes shut tight as hot white beams ripped through her, but she pulled them open in time to watch him unravel. His body bucking and jerking against her, he shoved his cock deeper, pushing harder and farther until his back curved into hers.

He pressed his lips between her shoulder blades, his warm breath dampening the skin under his loving kisses. Sweat set their bodies aglow under the darkening afternoon sky, and the only movement or sound between them was the pull of heavy breathing as they worked to regain their composure.

Still squat on her hands and knees, her arms began to tremble. He pulled away, scooped her into his arms and rolled against the bed, cradling her into his chest.

His breath still deep from climax, he brushed the hair from her neck and whispered in her ear, "You still got a problem with mirrors?"

She chuckled. "No. I think I'll keep the closet doors for a while."

He turned her to face him, and the look in his eyes stabbed at something deep inside her.

"You realize you've got nothing to be ashamed of." He used a finger to swipe a strand of hair from her face. "Everything about you is beautiful."

And with that one statement, with his soft, loving gaze and gentle caress, Carly realized she'd gone and done it.

She'd just fallen head over heels for Matt Jacobs.

14

MATT LAY ON HIS back in a dark, desolate room, fighting for air, the weight against his chest getting heavier, pressing harder with each passing moment. Blackness enveloped him. The only sound filling his ears was that of a lone bird chirping. He tried to move his arms, but they remained fastened in place by restraints he couldn't feel or see. He tried to cry out, but his voice was silent, his body frozen.

The vise around his chest tightened, weighing like bricks against his ribs, forcing his lungs to accept only slight shallow breaths. And as every moment passed, the vise clamped harder.

The bird chirped. He gasped for air, wishing desperately he could lash out in this blackened space and free himself from the bonds that held him captive. Air. He needed air. But the weight continued to press and squeeze against his breath. He felt a shroud coming over him, the dark mass of a life nearing its end, and just as he was certain he'd gulped in his last and final breath, his eyes flipped open.

He glanced around the room, the dark cloak clearing as he worked to find his bearings. This was Carly's bedroom, the lone chirping a bird calling from the purple plum tree outside the window at his right. It had been a dream, a weird, crazy dream, the remnants of which still weighed heavily on his chest.

Relieved yet still unsettled, he raised a hand to rub the

sleep from his eyes and bumped into something fuzzy. Startled, he looked down to find a ten-pound ball of gray fur rolled up on his chest.

Fricking cat!

He grabbed Mr. Doodles and tossed him off the side, the cat spouting out a complaint as it landed feetfirst on the floor. He held a hand to his ribs and took a deep breath, relief flooding through him when the air came in easily, no longer restrained by the weight of the animal.

Now he knew why he preferred dogs.

To his left, Carly slept soundly, her faced pressed against a pale blue pillow, long eyelashes fanned out over two rosy cheeks. Judging by the light from the window, he guessed it was early, the sun barely peeking over the hills to the east.

He propped up on his elbows and felt a thud at the base of the bed as Mr. Doodles jumped back up. The cat stopped near his feet and stared him down, obviously expecting Matt to lie back so he could return to his bare-chested bed.

Think again, Doodle dude.

The cat took a seat and waited. Matt lifted his lip and sneered. Doodles simply blinked.

Matt slipped back against the headboard and crossed his arms at his chest, letting the cat know the spot was gone.

Doodles licked a paw and waited, letting Matt know he had all day.

So much for sleeping in.

Dropping his feet to the floor, he went in search of his jeans, pulling them on and then finding his watch on the maple dresser. Seven-fourteen. Far too early for a Saturday morning, but he was awake now and intent on finding some strong, hot coffee. So he padded out of the bedroom with

Doodles at his feet, quietly closing the door behind him so at least one of them could get some sleep.

He passed her living room, picking up the pizza box and empty bottle of wine from the coffee table as he made his way toward the kitchen. Aside from a short pause for dinner, they'd spent the better part of the evening in bed, getting acquainted with a number of sexual fantasies Carly had dreamed up. Matt had been all too willing to assist her in playing each one of them out.

By the time they'd hit exhaustion they hadn't even tapped the list, leaving plenty more to get to. Maybe they'd do that today.

Stepping through the house and into the kitchen, he flicked on a light and began rummaging through the cupboards, tracking down coffee and filters, Doodle Dude making figure eights around his ankles every time he paused. Matt suspected the cat was after the half-empty can of cat food he'd seen in the refrigerator, and noting the empty dish near her tiny dinette, he popped it out and fed the cat his breakfast.

With the coffee brewing and Doodle Dude busy, Matt went to work cleaning up the mess from last night's dinner. He remembered seeing garbage cans lined up against her garage, so, picking up the empty pizza box, he stepped out the front door and headed down the rose-lined walkway.

A neighbor across the street, a woman who appeared to be in her midsixties, looked up from a bed of purple flowers and waved. Her warm, friendly eyes a pleasant but unexpected sight this early in the morning.

The condominium complex where Matt lived had stairs leading to separate garages, and despite the tight-knit quarters they all shared, he rarely saw any of his neighbors. Each unit backing up to the water, there were no shared open spaces for residents to gather and meet, and though he'd lived there for more than three years now, he couldn't name more than one or two of his neighbors.

By the looks of this short court, he guessed Carly knew everyone on the street. Each house was maintained with obvious care despite the age and modest size. This was a block that spoke of residents who took pride in their slice of America, and Matt knew that pride included looking out for each other.

He wondered how many of them would be chatting about *him* before the day was over.

Nodding, he smiled and returned a greeting before the woman went back to her flats of flowers and clumps of rich, fragrant dirt. After tossing the empty box, he stepped back inside to the luscious smell of fresh brewing coffee.

Carly's kitchen faced the front walkway. While Matt savored his first cup he took in the view from the window over her sink, the neighbor's flowers across the street, the Saab in the driveway next to it, a large play structure peeking from the backyard of the house to its right. Two homes had decorative flags attached to the garages, one of bright-colored flowers and the other a friendly Easter bunny, grinning well past his prime given they were heading toward June.

But still the sight warmed him, and he recalled a time he'd forgotten when he'd planned to someday have a family and a home of his own.

Back then his dreams included a house six times this size in a wealthy community like the ones a typical pro ballplayer lived in. When he made the big leagues and established himself as a regular, he was going to trade in his fetish for noncommittal women and look for a settling-down type. He hadn't wanted to get serious about a family until he'd accomplished the first of his dreams. And when that dream ended in the nightmare of defeat, he'd swept away those thoughts in the aftermath, never coming back to the idea again until this very moment.

Once his baseball career ended, he'd been too absorbed in despair and self-pity. And once he overcame that, he'd become consumed by his new career. Thoughts of a wife and family had been distant echoes of his past.

At least they had been before Carly.

Now, ever since that survey, since seeing this quirky little house she so desperately wanted as a home, ideas of love and family and futures had come full circle. And as he clutched the mug in his hands and stared out over this little slice of Mayberry, he had trouble shirking them off.

Having finished his meal, Mr. Doodles hopped up on the counter at Matt's side, the cat licked down a patch of fur, then came to rest near the sink. He stared up at Matt until Matt's softer nature prompted him to reach out and give the thing a pet.

He sort of liked this little place, even wondering for a moment if the large wealthy community of his old dreams would have really been the life he sought. Like Carly, he'd never had a real home, and in the cold, closed community of mansions and private drives, he wondered how happy he really would have been.

Life has a way of fixing things for us.

It was another of Stu's favorite phrases, and up until now Matt hadn't really swallowed its meaning. But gazing out into the calm, quiet morning, the phrase came back to him in this odd way he hadn't considered.

He stared down at the cat. "So what do you think, Doodle Dude? You like it here?"

The cat responded with a squeak, then rammed his head into Matt's side, demanding more of that petting thing he'd started. The sound of shuffling feet caught his attention, and he looked up toward the hallway to see Carly stepping into the kitchen wrapped in a fluffy white robe so big it seemed to consume her. Her lids were heavy, a crinkled sheet mark still etched across her cheek and her hair hanging in tufts about her face.

"I smell coffee," she said, lifting her chin to view the counter rather than open her eyes farther.

Matt pulled down a second mug. "What do you take in it?"

She shuffled to the refrigerator and pulled out a carton of milk. "Just this," she said.

With sleepy, robotic moves, she set down the milk, grabbed Mr. Doodles and plopped him to the floor as if this were a morning ritual they'd been sharing for some time now.

"I already fed him," he said.

Her only reply was a nod.

He smiled. "Not quite awake yet?" She shook her head and he topped her coffee with a splash of milk, then placed it in her hands. "Here. Maybe this will help."

She took a quick sip before setting the mug on the counter, choosing instead to wrap her fuzzy arms around his waist and bury her face in his chest. Taking a long, dragging breath, she hummed a sleepy groan of pleasure. "This is better."

He held her against him and kissed the top of her head. "Yes, it is."

"You don't have to leave, do you?"

He chuckled. "You want to continue what we started last night?"

"Yeah," she said, her voice muffled against his chest. "You?"

He set his mug next to hers, pulled her close and soaked in the fluffy feel of her, the strawberry essence of her hair and the warm press of her lips against his skin.

"Yes," he said. "Yes, I do."

"ARE WE GOING FOR our walk today?" Bev asked over the wall of Carly's cubicle.

Carly scoffed. "No way," she said. "It's supposed to be in the nineties today."

"You wimp."

"I'm not a wimp. I just don't think collapsing from heat exhaustion is a great way to spend my lunch hour." She grabbed a sprig of her hair and pulled it toward her face. "Besides, I got good curl in my hair this morning. One lap around the park will flatten it like a pancake."

"We're supposed to be getting fit."

Carly decided against reminding Bev that *she* was the one on the get-fit campaign. Carly had been getting enough exercise these last couple days between painting baseboards in her house and spending her evenings trying new acrobatics with Matt.

Instead she chose to state the obvious. "You can go without me, you know."

Bev mocked a laugh. "Yeah, right. Like that's going to happen." She stepped around the cubicle wall and took a seat at Carly's desk. "Okay, well, if I'm going to skip my exercise, I might as well go on a roll and have something bad for lunch. How about we go to Quimbly's? I haven't had a burger in weeks."

Carly shook her head. "Let's do something lighter. Matt's taking me out to dinner tonight to celebrate releasing the beta version of the new Singles Inc. site."

"Oh, fine. Ditch me so you can save yourself for your boyfriend."

"He's not my boyfriend."

"You've been inseparable ever since that weekend. I'd call that a boyfriend."

Carly reached in her drawer and pulled out her purse. "How about Sub Shack? It's two-for-one Friday."

Bev shrugged her acceptance and the two women headed for the restaurant, Bev agreeing that Carly had been right about the walk once they stepped out into the hot air. It was a rare day where the humidity was high, so both women were sweating by the time they covered the two blocks to the Sub Shack and stepped into the air-conditioned restaurant.

They made their way past the counter, Carly ordering her favorite sandwich—a vegetarian with Swiss cheese on a whole-wheat roll, coupled with a bag of sour-cream-and-onion potato chips and a Diet Coke. Bev picked a turkey club, insisting on at least splurging with bacon since she'd decided to blow her diet today.

Opting for a table in the corner, they sat down with their meals.

"Speaking of your boyfriend…" Bev said. "He's been the talk of the shop lately. Everyone's noticed his turnaround since the infamous blowup in the conference room. People are actually beginning to like him."

Carly rolled the paper off her sub and spread it out like a plate, ripping open her bag of chips and dumping them out next to her sandwich. "They should. He's a great guy."

Bev snorted. "It's still weird hearing you say that. You hated him for so long."

"I was wrong about him. We all were. Peel back the facade,

and there was a pretty nice guy underneath. He just needed a little prodding."

"He needed to be threatened with losing his job, you mean."

Carly huffed. "Must you be so cynical?" She popped a chip in her mouth. "I mean, yes, he made some mistakes when it came to getting along. Although all he needed was some help understanding how much better working can be when he pops out of that lab once in a while and lends a hand."

"Did you know he spent his entire afternoon yesterday in Fred's cube, helping him smooth out that animation for the Codding Bank site? It's actually pretty cool. Fred's been raving about it ever since."

"Yeah, Matt's doing a good job. Even Mr. Hall has commented about the difference in him. He's made quite the turnaround."

"Which means you've kept up your end of the bargain. So what has he done for *you* lately other than vastly improve your sex life?"

Carly frowned, not liking the sarcasm in Bev's tone. "He's done plenty," she snipped.

Bev held up a hand. "I'm not trying to be mean. I'm just wondering if Hall has said anything to you about your performance. I recall your deal with Matt was to help *each other* out."

"And he has." Though she had to think for a moment to come up with an example. "He's been making a big point to let Mr. Hall and Andy McGee know that I've done a lot of the design work. And he's shown me plenty of tricks along the way." She sipped her soda through a straw and set the large paper cup down. "He's worked very hard."

"Carly, I'm not saying he hasn't. It's just that I'm hearing a lot of buzz about Matt and not much about you. I worry how you might feel when he walks off with the management job."

"That hasn't been decided."

"But what's going to happen between you two when it is? I know you, Carly. You've got hearts in your eyes when it comes to him and you've conveniently forgotten that you two are competing for the same promotion. You've been spending a ton of time working with him, encouraging him to get to know the other designers, introducing him to the projects people are working on, insinuating him into the mix. You've done a great job helping him out." Bev gently clasped Carly's hand. "I just don't want you hurt when all your hard work gets him promoted over you."

"He hasn't gotten the job."

"But how would you feel if he did?"

Carly toyed with her paper napkin and pondered the question. "We agreed it would be a fair game. If he got promoted, I'd have no choice but to be happy for him."

"And in the end you'd be satisfied Matt did everything he could to help you as much as you've helped him?"

"Of course. We've been working together very well. I'm sure if there's more he could do for me, he would. There just hasn't been as much opportunity, that's all."

Bev shrugged and took a big bite out of the corner of her sandwich, giving Carly a moment to decide whether or not there was more she'd like to add to her defense.

Carly came up empty. What she'd said was true. Matt's problems on the job had been a lot easier to tackle than hers. She was charged with doing more to impress the client, and on a team project like Singles Inc. it was hard to express which one of them had done what. But as she'd said, on more than one occasion Matt had given her credit in front of the boss, making sure he'd played up her part in the design efforts.

"I'm only remembering that time after you read his survey—you'd walked away convinced he was a self-serving, egomaniacal jerk." Carly opened her mouth to object, but Bev cut her off. "I know you think you've seen a better side of him and I'm not saying he's not a good guy. I'm only wondering if you've considered the thought that he might be…" Bev shrugged rather than finishing the sentence.

Carly angrily filled in the blank. "He might be using me to get the job?"

"Weeks ago you would have been right here with me."

"Weeks ago I didn't know him the way I know him now."

"So all those survey answers were just a lie? What, was he in a bad mood that day or something?"

"I don't know. We've never discussed it."

Bev took an extended breath and gave Carly a look she didn't appreciate. It was a look that said she was being played the fool and was too infatuated to notice.

"We've never had to discuss it," she clarified. "I've got better instincts than that."

"Well, if I were you, I'd be asking him to explain all those answers. The man you've been describing lately doesn't sound anything like the guy who filled out those survey questions."

"Survey, schmurvey. That was ages ago. It's history."

"It was supposed to be a glimpse inside his personality, and if you recall, you hadn't liked what you'd seen."

"The man I know isn't the same man who filled out the survey."

"Are you sure?"

"Of course I'm sure."

And she was. A woman didn't spend practically every night with a man in the most intimate way possible without learning something about him. Around her, he was kind and caring, generous and tender. He'd helped her with her house and even put up with her cat. He had clothes at her house, she had clothes at his condo. That wasn't the type of thing a man did with a woman he was just using to get a job.

Yet, still, she didn't like the seed of doubt Bev had planted. Truth be told, Carly had completely forgotten about the survey. And, yes, maybe Matt was benefiting more from their pact than she was. And sure, she hadn't been immune to the office speculation that Matt would be the man heading up Mr. Hall's new design team.

She stared at her lunch, her interest in the sandwich dwindling by the minute.

"So if Matt does get that job, you won't feel cheated?" Bev asked. "You spent a lot of time upset that Hall kept passing you over for him. You could really just smile and say your congratulations to Matt if Hall does it again?"

Carly shrugged. "I don't have much choice, do I?"

"Not at this point in the game. You've already brought him up to speed on what he needed to do to land it. I'm only worried about how you'd take it if it happened."

Waving off the thread of doubt and suspicion Bev had fed her, Carly stiffened her spine and jutted her chin. "I'll feel he deserved it."

Bev looked surprised and impressed. "Then he's more special to you than I realized." She smiled, but it seemed more forced than genuine. "I'm happy for you. And who knows? You could be the one walking away with the job. That's highly possible, too." Then she took a sip of her soda and winked. "Then you can worry how *he's* going to take it."

15

"THIS IS BEAUTIFUL. I can't believe you don't sit out here more often."

Matt and Carly relaxed on the third-story balcony of his waterfront condominium in southern Marin, watching the sun settle over the hills to the west. The night sky was a bright shade of pink, turning deeper and more radiant as each minute passed.

Inside the double French doors was the master suite, where soft ballads wafted through the air from his bedroom stereo. Matt hadn't expected them to end up out here. The main living area was downstairs on the second floor over the two-car tandem garage that made up the ground level. This third floor only housed his master bedroom and a second room he used for storage.

After their dinner, he'd come up here to change, Carly following him for what he'd expected would be the typical nightcap of great sex that had become their regular habit. But one look at the bright pink sky and they'd found themselves on the balcony he never used, relaxing casually while they watched a rare beautiful sunset unhampered by the typical evening fog.

He took a swig of his beer. "Usually when I'm up here I'm either sleeping, showering or…busy." He shot her a wink.

She sank low in the cushy upholstered chair they'd stolen

from his bedroom and lazily watched the sunset. "I think it's good I don't have a view like this. I'd get lost in the beauty of it and never get anything done."

Matt looked toward the hills and the view he'd paid handsomely for, realizing that, aside from the day he'd first toured the condo and noticed the stunning skyline, he rarely, if ever, took the time to sit and enjoy it. That was, of course, before Carly. She had a way of stopping at every turn and making him see the obvious in front of him. Sunsets, kids playing in the park, a bright orange field of poppies—it was always something with her. She had a different way of looking at the world, and over these last few weeks, Matt had been enjoying seeing it through her eyes.

It was a positive vision, filled with hope and wonder. Where he'd spent a lifetime living in cynicism, being angry at most things and not caring to treasure the rest, Carly spent hers looking for the beauty in everything she crossed.

Including him.

He found her optimism contagious, her happiness a drug that soothed and warmed the tension from the day, and the more time he spent around her, the more he craved that dose of sunshine.

In front of them, the sky darkened to deep purple and then to smoky gray, when finally Carly clutched her arms and shivered, the warm evening turning chilly in typical San Francisco Bay fashion. Pulling from his chair, he held out a hand.

"Let's go in. Looks like the show's over."

Her bright eyes darkened to something seductive. "I need warming up."

They stepped inside and he closed the doors behind him, and within seconds they'd shed their clothes and landed under the covers of his oversize bed. Her skin was gooseflesh, her nipples puckered from cold, and he spooned her against him to bring heat back through her veins.

Her hair felt like satin against his chest, her body folding into his with that perfect fit that felt made just for him. Smothering his hands over her until she warmed in his embrace, he soaked in her very essence, trying to remember a time when he was this at peace with his heart and his life. Only back in the early days before his parents' divorce, back before his father dismissed him and his mother grew bitter, had he known this kind of inner tranquility. It felt good but only vaguely familiar, comforting and unsettling all at once, and as he held her close he tried to reconcile the mix of emotions that had begun rattling his sense of security. He'd been feeling it for days, not sure what to do with it or where to place it in the tidy world he'd built for himself.

She turned in his arms and pressed a cold nose against his chest. "I had an idea."

Carly had a lot of ideas. Sometimes he wondered if she spent half her day thinking up new things to do with him in bed.

Not that he was complaining.

"What have you come up with *this time?*"

She looked up at him, clearly put off. "*Well.* If my ideas are growing old with you, I can always call it a night." He caught her playful smile just before she rolled over and began fluffing her pillow.

He rolled her back. "Nothing about you is ever going to get old with me." Then he closed his mouth over hers.

She sank back against the pillow, and he slipped his hands around her waist, pulling her hips against a fast-growing erection. Almost nightly sex and still he hadn't begun to whet his appetite for this woman, his body feeling almost abandoned when it wasn't enveloped in hers. It was a strange phenomenon for a man who used to bore easily and tended to get itchy when people got too close. With Carly, his only itch was a constant need for her, and as he began kissing a path down her neck, he considered the many ways he might scratch it.

"I want to hear your idea," he muttered against her shoulder.

She whispered something about vibrators and that cozy chair they'd left out on the balcony, and while intrigued, Matt wasn't in the mood to leave the bed and go fetch it. In fact, at the moment he was overcome with a need to simply hold her in his arms and sink between her legs. Tonight the notoriety of wild and kinky sex had a cheapness to it he couldn't put into words, and while he enjoyed their common fetish, he felt a sudden urge to get right inside her where they were. To take her straight and close, where he could slip into her gaze and watch her blossom beneath him.

Rolling her onto her back, he moved over her, nudging her thighs apart and resting his hips between them. He cupped her face in his hands and studied the pleasured look of anticipation in her eyes, then spoke through a series of kisses.

"I like that idea," he said, nudging his cock against her slick core. "But tonight I think I'd like this better." Then he slid inside, her eyes lolling shut as his thick shaft filled her.

He closed his mouth over hers, shoving his tongue far inside, and when he did, something seemed to snap deep within him.

Nestling his body into hers, a driving need began to build, a need to consume, to dig in and grab hold of some piece of her he could hang on to. Suddenly sex didn't feel like enough. Simply pleasuring her felt too slight for the ache in his chest, and he clasped one hand against her ass, arching her into him to drive this desire deeper.

And it wasn't enough.

As he moved over her, caressing his hands over her hot flesh, stroking his cock through her core, sucking and tasting every spot his mouth could reach, a growing hunger formed in his chest. A hunger so deep and tragic he didn't know how to feed it. It swelled with every stroke, with every press of his lips to hers, and he quickened the pace, thrusting harder and deeper, hoping speed and force might quench the thirst.

Her breath came out in pants, her eyes growing delighted as he tightened his grip on her and tried to pull her closer. He felt like a speeding train, gaining momentum yet spinning out of control with no way to stop the force.

He felt an aching need for release, for some sort of finality, but with every stroke the yearning only grew.

Sweat broke out on his skin and he raised himself, bracing against the mattress to drive harder, deeper and faster. Carly's face flushed, her expression a mix of pain and bliss. Grunts escaped her chest with every hard thrust, and in a sudden breath of panic he asked, "Am I hurting you?"

She shook her head and gripped her hands around his wrists. "Don't stop," she panted. "Go, go."

He lost the air in his lungs, pleasure swelling between his legs but the thirsty void in his chest only grew with every thrust. He wanted to come fast and hard, thinking only a searing release might stop the torment, and the faster he moved, the higher he crested.

Her fingers dug into his wrists, need seared in her eyes, a sharp cry spilling from her throat each time he slapped deep against her. And every time he feared he was humping too hard, she simply cried out, "Harder."

His legs trembled, his muscles burned. Underneath him Carly arched and curved, trying to greet the force thrust by thrust. His cock ached to the point of pain, the strain nearly splitting him apart, and just as he began to fear the fierce climax edging to the surface, she threw her head back and cried out in searing release.

He instantly followed, their bodies jerking and buckling as he spilled himself inside her. The waves were cresting hard and fast, crashing against him one right after the other until there was nothing left of him to give. The climax split so quickly it hurt, her hot body clamping tight around him as she reached to his chest and dug her fingers in the flesh. Friction mounted, more waves trickled through him, finally slowing and easing until he collapsed next to her. Scooping her tightly in his arms, he pressed his face against her chest and squeezed his eyes shut to the sensation.

"Oh, wow," she gasped. "That was incredible."

But Matt couldn't answer. Something inside him had broken open, something frightening and foreign yet comforting and warm. And as he held her damp body in his arms and clutched her like he couldn't let go, he understood what had happened.

He'd fallen desperately in love.

ADAM STOOD IN Matt's new office and whistled. "Wow, these are some upscale digs."

Matt couldn't argue. Sitting in the center of a mahogany U-shaped desk ensemble, the large leather executive chair cushy at his back, he felt a bit like a king.

Even given the size of his desk, there was still space in the office for a mahogany conference table and four upholstered chairs, a matching couch and two club chairs. One entire wall provided a view of Lakeford Park, and after watching Carly ogle it, he'd acknowledged not every manager in this business got treated so well.

Heck, at Web Tactics managers only got a slightly bigger cubicle and a modest pay increase. But Hall knew how to retain the people he wanted and had never dismissed the appeal of money and perks. For two years Matt had been staring at these empty offices wishing one of them would be his, and finally it had happened.

Now if he could only be happy about it.

"This is amazing," Carly said, then she lowered her voice. "I think this is nicer than Frank's office. The furniture is newer, for sure."

Though she was putting up a good front, Matt could see that something in her eyes had changed. There was a hardening to her stance, a protectiveness, as if she'd put up a shield of defense expecting things between them to change.

He definitely wanted things between them to change, but not in the way she expected.

For over a week Matt had been planning a special evening for the two of them where he would profess his love for her and talk about their futures, but before he could arrange it, Hall had announced his promotion and turned his world on end. Every day and night the man had been at his side, making plans and barking orders, filling every instant with meetings and arrangements. Matt expected that things would be hectic for the moment, but what he hadn't expected was the feeling that somehow he and Carly were being pulled apart, and he feared that even a profession of love wouldn't put things back together.

"Has Frank seen it?" Adam asked.

"He stopped in a few minutes ago," Carly replied. "He didn't have much to say."

"He'll get over it," Matt said. "After all, he was the one with the new office once. It's a rite of passage."

Moving to the door, Adam stopped at the threshold. "Well, congratulations again, buddy. We're all happy for you." Then he added before leaving, "You need some accessories. That one Chinese take-out menu you had tacked to your cube isn't going to hack it in the big office."

"Yeah, I'll get right on it."

And then he and Carly were alone, Matt stuck with that pit of discomfort he'd felt ever since Hall had promoted him. Getting this big office was supposed to have righted everything wrong in his life. He'd wanted to be the best at something, to climb to the top of his field and bask in the view with a sense of pride and satisfaction. And more importantly, he'd wanted to outscore his old man.

Though Jeff Jacobs made a decent living selling insurance, Matt had officially surpassed that career with this leap onto executive row, and this was the moment Matt had always believed would reconcile his soul. He'd needed this. He'd needed this confirmation, proof that if he tried, he could be better than the stock he came from. But instead of having glory, it all felt empty.

Because, since falling in love with Carly, Jeff Jacobs wasn't the person he cared to prove himself to anymore.

"So," Carly said. "What time will you be by tonight?"

"Tonight?"

She frowned. "Dinner with my mother?"

He winced. He knew there was something he was supposed

to have handled this afternoon. "I'm sorry, hon, but Brayton called a late meeting tonight."

She couldn't hide the disappointment in her eyes despite the shrug and forced smile. "That's okay. I'll see you tomorrow, then, for Jodi's game."

His wince deepened. Why hadn't he told her this before? "He made a golf date, too. The man's tied me up all weekend."

Lifting her chin, she worked to hold up the good front, but it was long from reaching her eyes. "That's okay."

"Carly, I'm sorry. He's assured me these are just last-minute meetings to get me acquainted with some of the associates he works with. In a week or two things will all be back to normal and I'll be on a regular work schedule."

"Matt, if it was only me, I wouldn't care. I just hate disappointing Jodi. She gets enough of that already."

That one hurt.

He pushed up and rounded his desk, clutching her shoulders and trying to ignore the feeling that everything was slipping out from under him like sand through a sieve. "Honey, I said I was sorry. I don't plan to make a habit of breaking promises, but you've got to cut me a break. I was just promoted and things are shaken up right now. Soon this will all settle and things will be like they always were."

Her brow twitched at that statement, but she quickly covered it over with a sigh and a smile. "You're right and I do understand. Jodi will, too." Then she tipped to her toes and touched her lips to his cheek. "Get yourself settled in the new job and we'll pick up where we left off."

Pick up where they'd left off? He'd left off in a space where life felt good being in love with the woman of his dreams. Now it was all falling apart, and he didn't know what to do to right it.

Dammit, he'd earned this promotion. He hadn't lied to her or anyone else. Was he supposed to walk in to Hall and turn it down? Would it make Carly happy knowing she only got a promotion because Hall's first choice had opted out? He knew her better than that. Her pride wouldn't let her accept it.

She stepped out of his office and Matt went back to his big, shiny desk. He plopped into his chair feeling trapped without options. He'd thought they'd done the right thing when making that pact. For weeks they'd worked together, knowing this day would come and that one of them would lose. He thought Carly had been prepared for this. Everyone speculated he'd be the one to get the job, and up until it happened, she'd seemed fine with it.

So why did it now feel as if their relationship was coming to an end?

16

CARLY WENT BACK to her cubicle and slipped into her chair, the walls feeling suffocatingly tight after being in the spacious surroundings of Matt's new office. For days now she'd been trying hard to be happy for him, to be the good loser, knowing they both couldn't get the job. She would have wanted Matt to be happy for her if the tables were turned.

But darn it if she couldn't shake off the feeling she'd been played the fool. As much as she wanted to deny it, as much as she kept replaying every loving thing Matt had done for her over the last several weeks—his tender kisses and gentle words—a knot in her stomach wouldn't dismiss the fact that she hadn't spent one evening with him since he'd gotten the new job.

And it all felt too convenient.

Bev's warning came back to her, the notion that though they'd made a pact, Matt had gotten way more out of the deal than Carly had. She'd turned it over a dozen times, trying to justify the situation until she'd run out of excuses, and she kept coming back to the same space. She'd been supportive, helpful and kind, and Matt had walked away with the job she still felt she deserved. In fact, all her hard work hadn't gotten her anything but a pat on the back from her traitorous boss and shoved aside by the man she loved.

She checked her watch and grabbed her purse, deciding to

call it a day. Without Matt going along, she could go straight to her mother's apartment and distract herself by dinner with her family. So she headed out the door and stepped into another hot summer evening. She took a deep breath, wanting the sultry air to burn off these feelings of loss and abandonment. It was hard not to overreact, to hold on to hope that what Matt said was true, that he'd been distant and distracted because Hall had been running him crazy lately. She'd seen that for herself. Maybe it was possible things would go back to normal once the newness settled down.

But the angry thorn in her side said nothing would be normal again, because no matter what happened with her and Matt, he was a new manager and she was still one of the working stiffs.

She clicked the button on her key chain to unlock the door to her Grand Prix. Stepping behind the wheel, she began making her way to her mother's place, her fate feeling dimmer with every mile she drove. The handwriting was on the wall for her at Hall Technologies. Obviously Mr. Hall didn't feel she was management material, and despite her situation with Matt, she had to face the reality that she'd hit the glass ceiling at her current job. Though it was a fast-growing company, it was apparently growing without her, and if Mr. Hall thought he could hold on to her forever as a tried and true workhorse, he was in for a rude awakening.

Speeding up the freeway, she thought about updating her résumé and beginning the search for a new job. She had a friend at an employment agency who could help her find openings, and though she might not get the salary she was making now, at least she'd walk away feeling empowered, reminding herself that she was the one in control of her career, not Brayton Hall.

She liked that idea and the sense of freedom it gave her. Until the thought of not seeing Matt every day pulled the weight back onto her shoulders. It lodged a lump in her throat and stung the backs of her eyes.

God help her, she loved him, and as much as it hurt thinking he'd only used her to get the promotion, the idea of never seeing him again hurt more. It crushed against her chest and quivered her chin, and by the time she got to her mother's apartment she'd managed to work herself into a complete and total state of misery.

Pulling into the complex, she saw that a midnight-blue Mercedes with shiny new Nevada plates was parked in the spot she usually took, so she rounded the lot and parallel parked on the street instead. She was a bit early, but given this was her mother's day off work, she knew her mom would be there and there'd be something she could help with before dinner.

At least twice a month Carly tried to spend some time with her mom and Jodi, often bringing Jodi back to her house for a sisters-only sleepover. With fourteen years between them, they'd both nearly been raised as only children, and she knew how much Jodi treasured the time they spent doing sisterly things.

She used her key to let herself in, only to be greeted by the sound of her father's voice.

"There's my girl!" he called out, pulling up from the couch and moving to the entryway to surround her in a bear hug.

Carly was taken aback. The man had been gone four months, longer than he usually stayed away without so much as popping in for a weekend, and a side of her had thought this time he might not be coming back. Her father sold vacation property, his business taking him wherever there were new developments popping up. From what she understood, he was licensed to sell real estate all over the western half of the United States, and if that were the case, Carly didn't understand why he couldn't make a lucrative career selling homes around here. The agents she knew were doing well for themselves, none of them needing to spend weeks and months away from their families in order to make a living.

And none of them leaving their wives and daughters nearly broke and having to fend for themselves.

There was way more to the story than she'd ever know, and for the most part she'd stopped asking. Her mother was a fool in love, and she supposed, when looking at David Abrams objectively, Carly couldn't blame her.

The man was strikingly good-looking, with vivid blue eyes, thick salt-and-pepper hair and a strong jaw and nose reminiscent of a Roman warrior. In many ways he reminded her of Matt, and the irony of the situation wasn't lost on Carly. She was finding herself quickly trailing in the path of her mother if she allowed her life to go that way.

He pulled from the embrace and clasped his hands to her shoulders. "I think you've gotten more beautiful since I saw you last."

She tried to stretch her mouth into a smile, when Jodi jumped up behind him. "Dad's home! And look what he brought me!"

Jodi spun around, her long brown hair whipping around like a horse's tail, her pink-and-yellow sundress twirling at her waist. And on her back was a bright purple backpack.

"Oh," Carly said, forcing the annoyance from her tone. "A purple backpack."

He placed an affectionate hand on Jodi's head and gave it a rub. "Carol said she needed one. I found that in an outlet mall just outside Vegas." He accepted another hug from his youngest daughter. "Is that what you were hoping for, sweetheart?"

Carly seethed, not at all in the mood for dealing with any of this today. Life had already gotten bad enough without her father stepping in. She'd hoped a nice evening and some motherly advice might improve things, but instead David Abrams had shown up and worsened it.

"I still love the one *you* gave me," Jodi said to Carly. "This will be my school bag and I'll use yours for camps."

"Oh, and I've got something for you, too," their father said, pulling out a velvet box and placing it in Carly's hands. She opened it, and inside was a tennis bracelet as sparkly and shiny as the smile on his face.

It was classic David Abrams. Her mother had a jewelry box filled with things like this, none of it coming in handy when tuition was due or the rent was late.

She feigned acceptance for the sake of keeping peace, but it burned that her father could waltz in with the wind, throw presents around and make everyone swoon. Where had he been when she was driving all over Marin trying desperately to find her sister exactly what she wanted? What was he doing when her mother was sick but still pulling herself through finals on top of taking care of his daughter? And if he was such a master at selling real estate, why was his family living in this shabby little apartment?

She stopped and stared as a chafing thought popped in her mind. "Is that your Mercedes out there?"

He grinned. "Nice, huh?"

"Did you know Mom's Toyota has over two hundred thousand miles on it?"

On that note, Carly's mother whisked from the kitchen with a plate of cheese and crackers. "Let's go sit down. I'm sure everyone's hungry."

Carol Abrams was a woman who looked young for her age, she and Carly often being mistaken for sisters. In her jeans and tight sleeveless T-shirt, Carly knew she could have a dozen men interested in taking her out, yet she sat here in this dingy apartment trying to make ends meet while she stayed forever faithful to this man she called a husband. It was a situation Carly would never, ever understand.

Dropping the bracelet in her purse, she followed them into the small living room.

"I didn't know it had gotten that old," her father said. "We'll have to take care of that."

"The Mercedes must have cost a fortune," Carly said, ignoring the look of scorn in her mother's eyes. *Someone* had to stick up for the family. Carol Abrams surely didn't.

"Now, Carly, I know what you're thinking, but to make money in my business I've got to spend it. No one's going to buy a lakefront estate from someone driving around in a rust bucket."

Carly took a seat at the small dining table that made up half of the living room. "And exactly what lake are you selling?"

Her father rolled up the sleeves on his tailored dress shirt, then rested an arm on the back of the sofa. "We just wrapped up a new subdivision out near Vegas. Now I'm heading up to Shastina."

"That's five hours from here."

He grinned. "I know. I'll finally be able to start coming home on weekends."

Weekends. How lucky for them.

She spent the rest of the evening trying to put on a good face for the sake of her mother and Jodi, deciding not to ruin a night with Dad by pointing out the obvious to everyone in the room. In Carly's eyes, there was no way a handsome man like David Abrams would spend four months of celibacy—*in Vegas, no less*—being true to the woman he ignored. And while she'd long ago lost respect for her father, she'd never accept why a bright, attractive woman like her mother put up with it.

It wasn't until the next day when she showed up for Jodi's softball game and her father was once again absent that the lid blew off Carly's restraint.

"Where is he?" she asked her mother.

Her mother shrugged flippantly. "He just had to run some errands. He said he wouldn't miss Jodi's game. He promised."

"It's the third inning. When are you going to stop letting him make promises to Jodi you know he won't keep?"

"This isn't the time or place," Carol said, resting a hand on Carly's thigh.

Carly lowered her voice. "Jodi keeps looking up here. If he doesn't appear before the end of the game, she's going to be devastated. *Again.*"

"Jodi will be fine," her mother assured, and it was the last thing Carly could take before she snapped.

"No, she won't be fine. None of us will be fine."

Confusion, resentment and frustration clamped around her throat, and she shot up from the bleachers and stormed out to the parking lot. The week had finally caught up to her to the extent that she couldn't handle any more. She wanted to step back in time, back when things were good and she was happy in love, sharing her days and nights with Matt. She wanted him here right now, calming her nerves, whispering sweet assurances and helping her gain perspective on this life that kept throwing her curveballs at every turn.

But just like her father, Matt wasn't here. Instead he was on a golf course, advancing the career that should have been hers. And later, when he was having cocktails at the nineteenth hole, she'd be consoling her sister after the other man in her life let them down again.

Anger boiled in her chest and tears of loss singed her eyes as she stepped to her mother's beat-up Toyota and leaned against the hood.

Why had she let herself fall in love with him? She knew from the moment she met Matt Jacobs he was destined to break her heart. The survey hadn't lied. It had spelled out exactly the kind of man she was dealing with, but somewhere in all the confetti she'd let that fact escape her mind. How could she have forgotten? What had she actually thought would happen once he took the management job and didn't need her anymore?

"Carly, what's gotten into you?" Her mother came up behind her and placed a hand on her shoulder. "Why are you so upset? Your father said he'd be here, and he will."

She spun around, hurt and ire spilling from her eyes and fisting around her chest. "No, he won't. It will be just like always. He's got an excuse, something came up. It's the same thing he always does. He waltzes in with presents, throws money around for a minute, then walks out to spend the next four months doing what *he* wants."

"He's got to make a living, Carly."

"And he can't do that and have a family at the same time?"

"He does have a family, we just have to make sacrifices on occasion. That's how families get along."

"But why are *we* the ones doing all the sacrificing? What

is *he* missing out on? While we do all the work, he walks in and grabs the credit, and in the end we're supposed to smile and be grateful we helped him make it to the top." The more she spoke, the angrier she became. "Just once I'd like to see him sacrifice something for me. Prove to me I haven't been the stooge all along, working to get him promoted." Tears rolled down her cheeks and she couldn't catch her breath. "God, he hasn't even so much as taken me out to dinner. I'm the one who put him there—and where is he? Playing golf with his new executive cronies."

"Carly, what on earth are you talking about?" Her mother's eyes grew dark and concerned.

"Dad! Where do you think he is right now? Poor Jodi's there in the dugout, praying her father will watch her bat, and where is he?"

"Honey, you're confusing me."

Carly's chest heaved, her eyes blurred. "How could I be so stupid? I saw it right on his survey. He's just like Dad. He's exactly like Dad. I even thought that to myself when I sat in Bev's den and read the survey. How could I have just slid that under the rug?"

Her mother grabbed her shoulders. "Carly, what are you talking about? What survey?"

She stopped and stared.

"Matt, Mom. He got the promotion and I've barely seen him since." Saying it out loud released another wave of tears, and she clutched her mother and buried her face in her chest. "It's just like Bev said. He was only using me to get the job."

Her mother held her tight. "Oh, Carly. Is that what he said?"

"He doesn't have to. It's all playing out like I feared. He got my job, he got the big cushy office, and I'm left with nothing."

"Now, wait a minute," Carol said, holding her daughter close but nudging them toward a park bench. "You aren't making sense. Sit down and tell me what happened."

Carly did, starting with the survey and going from there. She told her about the management job opening and how she and Matt had both been in the running, about their agreement to work together and even the loving time they'd spent in each other's arms. And then she detailed the events of the last week, how he'd been planning to meet her family, how excited Jodi had been about meeting a real baseball player and how it all fell apart the moment he got the job.

And when she was done she felt tired and spent, as if a lifetime of dreams and failures had just played out in front of her.

"I think you need to have a little more patience," her mother said. "It's like you said—he just got promoted. It's a stressful time for him and he needs to focus on that. It doesn't mean he's stopped caring for you."

Of course her mother would think that. Carol Abrams was faithful to a fault, their whole family suffering because of her staunch belief in the good of human nature.

Carly had always sworn she'd never be so foolish, and in a way she felt compelled to do the opposite of whatever advice her mom tried to dole out, wanting to make sure she didn't end up in the same place twenty-six years from now.

"Why do you do it, Mom?" she asked. "Doesn't it ever cross your mind Dad's cheating on you?"

"I have to have faith in our vows, Carly. Without that, a marriage is nothing."

"Mom, don't be stupid."

Her mother held up a hand the same way she always did when Carly went down this path, but this time Carly saw things differently. She'd had a taste of a man like her father, and as exciting as Matt was, as thrilling as he'd been to be with, she could never play second fiddle in his life the way her mother did in her dad's.

"I know he's not the father you wanted."

"Is he the husband you wanted?" she asked.

Carol cocked a crooked smile. "I don't have a choice. I fell in love with him and I've never fallen out. Besides," she said, staring off toward the football field in the distance, "I knew what I was getting into when I married him."

"He's always been like this?"

"He could never settle down. And all I have to do is say the word and he would take me with him wherever he went. But I didn't want that for you and Jodi." She eyed her daughter, for the first time explaining this strange relationship of hers. "It's my choice to stay here in one place, not his. If I said so, we'd all be living as a family and probably much better off without the added expense of maintaining two households. But your father's not going to change, and I never wanted you girls to have to move around along with him. So this is the compromise we made."

It shed some light on the situation but did little to help Carly's opinion of him. "And he couldn't make sacrifices to keep us together as a family? Would it really kill the guy to make a living in one place for a while?"

Carol bit her lip and darted her eyes. "It's like I said, Carly. I knew what I was getting into when I married him."

Carly looked across the large grassy field where dozens of little boys in oversize shoulder pads were getting ready for Pop Warner football. And as she watched she realized she'd been given the same view of Matt. She'd read his survey, she'd known exactly who she was dealing with and what she was getting into. The survey hadn't lied and neither had he. She'd simply been her mother's child, the fool in love who'd turned her back to the grim reality and hoped somewhere it would have all played out differently.

But it hadn't. Life turned out exactly as she should have expected all those weeks ago, and it was silly, really, to be sitting here shocked and dismayed in the aftermath.

It wouldn't have taken a psychic to figure out that Matt was destined to walk away with the job and she was destined to end up with nothing. And as she sat here in the sisterhood of another woman who'd lost her heart to the wrong man, Carly went back to the promise she'd made to herself years ago.

Love or not in love, she wasn't going to end up like her mother.

17

MATT WALKED INTO the Dugout only three minutes late, having had to duck out of the office in order to keep his meeting with Tommy, the boy he'd been helping with batting lessons. After the golf game Saturday, Hall had pulled him along for the weekend, entertaining prospective clients and keeping Matt at his side until late last night. He'd wanted to meet up with Carly, try to make things right between them, but every chance he'd had to call her she'd cut him off short.

And this morning seeing her in person hadn't gone much better.

Truth was, she was pulling away from him, creating a valley between them he couldn't seem to cross, and with every moment that passed more and more he feared he might not get her back again.

That was one problem he'd been dealing with, the second being keeping up with Hall's new schedule without letting down his new student. He'd literally run from the office, disregarding an electronic calendar invite for yet another meeting in order to keep this lesson with Tommy. Job or no job, Matt wasn't going to let the kid down.

He rushed up the old wood stairs to the cages and pro shop, expecting to see Tommy sitting at their favorite table next to the Gatorade machine, but the table was empty.

Stu's daughter, Patsy, called from behind the counter. "Tommy had to cancel. Orthodontist appointment. Didn't you get the message?"

Matt's shoulders slumped. "No, I haven't had a chance to check my messages today."

Patsy smiled apologetically. "Yeah, well, he said he'd see you next week at the regular time."

Matt slipped into a chair and ran a hand over his face. He wanted to catch his breath after the mad rush here and decided, as a consolation, he had an hour to kill before returning to the chaos Hall had been keeping him in.

"Dad's in the cages if you want to say hi," Patsy said. "He's recalibrating machine number three."

Stu could spend his life recalibrating that machine and those balls would still threaten to take a guy's head off. Someday Matt was going to buy Stu some new machines.

Stepping down the aisle of cages, he popped into the third one, being careful to stay near the fence as he made his way toward the machine. When Stu worked on the machines, one never knew when a random ball would come flying out like a fat rubber bullet. He grabbed a metal folding chair on his way and took a seat next to Stu's feet—the only part of him visible from behind the machine.

"I'm glad you're here," Stu said, and Matt wondered if Stu even knew it was him. "Hand me the three-sixteenths."

A greasy hand popped out in waiting, and Matt looked down to the red metal toolbox at their feet. He reached in, assuming a three-sixteenths was one of these wrenches, each one an exact replica of the other. He began sorting through them, looking for some sort of sign, when he heard Stu's impatient huff. "The one with the white paint splatter."

Matt held it up like an Olympic torch, then placed it in Stu's waiting hand, and within seconds a fastball went shooting out of the machine with enough speed to split an atom.

"You might want to slow it down," Matt droned.

The next ball thumped out and hit the ground three feet from the machine, rolling lazily to the center thanks to the slant in the floor.

"Somewhere in between would be my suggestion."

The three-sixteenths went flying end over end, and Matt ducked.

"Dang blasted machine!" Stu called out.

"Someday I'm buying you a new one."

Scooting out from behind the equipment, Stu hung an Out of Order sign on the front and turned to Matt. "With that new fancy job of yours, I just might let you." They gathered up the tools, then headed back to Stu's office, Matt stopping for his customary Dr Pepper before taking a seat in front of Stu's old metal desk circa 1943.

"How is that new job of yours, by the way?" Stu asked.

"Busier than I expected. My sessions with Tommy have been the only chance I've had to get away from the job in over a week."

Stu stepped into the small bathroom off the side of his office and turned the tap on the sink. "Well, I'm sure your boss wants to get his money's worth, what with the big pay increase."

Matt propped his feet on a spare chair. "Yeah, and I wouldn't mind so much if it wasn't putting such a strain on me and Carly."

"Ah, well, the easy part's falling in love. The hard part's making it work over the long haul." Stu grabbed a bar of soap and began lathering his hands.

"She doesn't understand what this job is like," Matt said over the rush of the running water. "She thinks I'm giving her the brush-off, but I'm not. Hall's been running me ragged and I haven't had a moment to spend with her."

"Yeah?" Stu used his elbow to shut off the tap while he worked the foam over his fingers and nails. "Funny, you haven't missed your sessions with Tommy."

"Stu, you know I'm not going to let the kid down. As it was I had to dodge a meeting this afternoon to get here. I didn't even stop to check my voice mails today to find out he'd gone and canceled on me."

"And as busy as you are, you still showed up. Somehow you made the time."

"You know why I won't let him down." Stu had known Matt long enough to know he'd move mountains before he canceled out on a session with a young kid. Matt had been there too many times, had known how demeaning it felt being passed over by people who were supposed to be there for him.

"So why can't you make the time with Carly?"

Matt opened his mouth to answer, then suddenly found he didn't have one.

Stu peeked through the open door. "Seems to me you've gotten *some* of your priorities straight. You're willing to put a kid you barely know ahead of your job, which is an admirable thing. Now where's your priorities when it comes to this woman you seem to care so much about?"

When Matt didn't answer, Stu flicked on the faucet and rinsed his hands, then grabbed a towel and stepped into the office. "You know, Matt, we don't always have to make a choice between a rock and a hard place, but we should know which one we'd pick if we had to." He took a seat behind his desk and tossed the paper towel in the trash. "If you had to choose between your new job or your new girl, do you know which one you'd take?"

It was a good question, one Matt continued to turn over as he finished his drink and wrapped up his visit with Stu.

As he headed back to the office he knew Stu had been right. Matt had managed to make time for Tommy despite the frantic schedule Hall had him on, yet he hadn't made it as high a priority to set aside time for Carly. He'd just figured Carly was an adult and should understand, while Tom was a kid who wouldn't.

Or was he merely making an excuse for himself?

Maybe a side of him hadn't wanted to press things with Carly because he'd been afraid of the response he'd get. He knew she wasn't happy with him. He could see that in her eyes, hear it in her tone and feel it under his skin. As much as both of them tried to deny it, she'd felt he'd used her, and he simply couldn't find the words that would prove to her he hadn't.

Stepping back in the office, he was grateful to discover that Hall was tied up in meetings, giving Matt some badly needed time to sit down and pull his thoughts together. Somehow he had to find a way to let her know that he loved her, and not just because of what she'd done for him on the job. He had to make her understand he would have loved her even if he hadn't gotten the promotion. But how could he do that now that the deed was done?

"I found this in the back of your desk drawer. Do you need it?"

He looked up and saw Melissa Avery, the programmer who'd moved into his old cubicle. Reaching out, he took the notebook in her hand. "Sure, thanks," he said as she walked out the door.

It was the leather-bound notepad he thought he'd lost, and, opening the cover, he saw his Singles Inc. code name and password he'd jotted down all those weeks ago. The last time he'd used this was during the meeting with Hall on the project.

The project that started this mess.

He moved to rip the page from the pad, when something hit him, and instead of throwing the paper away, he turned to his laptop and logged into the site, curious to see if their survey results were still in the database. Sure enough, once he keyed in his user information his results popped up before him, and he began looking over the answers.

And before he got halfway through he saw his problems clearly before him.

He didn't recognize the cynical man behind all these answers. He'd come so far in the last few weeks, looking at his life differently, seeing the world through Carly's eyes and through the light she'd brought to his. No wonder he'd scored so low with everyone in the group. This survey painted him as a regular ass.

And in all honesty, back when he'd filled it out, that's exactly what he was.

Cynical, self-absorbed, egotistical. Answer after answer drew a picture of a man who cared only about himself. To the point where he hadn't been concerned enough to answer the questions with any sincerity. Admittedly, most of this didn't even reflect the man he'd been at the time. He'd been annoyed back then, feeling the survey was a stupid gimmick Hall had concocted, and many of his responses spoke to that state of mind.

He'd scoffed at much of it and toyed with the rest, only the part about sex being the section he'd given care to—and even then only because he'd found the questions amusing.

Shaking his head, he sighed. No wonder Carly had been so quick to brush him off in those early days of the project. Given this image of him, he wondered how she'd even built up enough trust to get along with him.

And then he stared at the screen as that last thought struck him like a slap in the face.

This damned survey. Carly had read his answers, and despite what she'd seen, she'd placed her trust with him anyway. And what she got was passed over for a promotion by a man this survey painted as a selfish, arrogant child.

He fell back against the chair and stared at the screen. This wasn't him, but he'd bet this was the man Carly feared she'd grown to care for. And since his promotion he'd done nothing to prove otherwise.

He rubbed his face in his hands as this all became so clear in front of him. He needed to show her this wasn't him, and, as his unconscious kept trying to tell him, he wouldn't be able to show her with words. He had to truly convince her she hadn't gone wrong by trusting him. She'd supported him when he'd needed it most, helped him fulfill his dream, and now it was his turn to repay her and set things right.

Stuck between a rock and a hard place. That was damn straight. But with Stu's words still echoing through his mind, he knew there was only one choice to make.

BRAYTON HALL SAT behind his desk, his hands folded on the tabletop, his eyes focused intently on Matt and Carly.

Since calling this meeting an hour ago, he'd refused to tell Carly what it was about, but based on the confident gleam in Matt's eyes, she suspected he knew something. He looked like the cat that caught the canary, entirely smug, as if he were bursting with good news, which left her entirely confused. If her conversation with Mr. Hall this morning had made it to his ears, she would have hoped for something different.

For what seemed like an exasperatingly long moment

Brayton only sat and stared at the two of them, not saying anything, until he finally cleared his throat and began.

"Now that I've managed to get the two of you together," he said, "let me start off this meeting by informing you that neither of you is quitting."

Her eyes collided with Matt's. "You quit!" they said in unison.

"Technically, Matt stepped down from his new position," Brayton said. "But I'm not letting that happen, either."

Carly gaped at Matt, who returned her expression with mirrored confusion.

"Apparently, Matt thinks if he steps down from the job, I'll promote you in his place," Brayton explained.

Carly inhaled a breath, and Matt reached out to take her hand, his eyes speaking a million words he couldn't say in front of Mr. Hall. And Carly didn't need to hear them. She knew what he'd done, and as it began to sink in, a rush of tears threatened to surface in front of the boss.

Or the ex-boss.

She'd already given her resignation. Having made the painful decision that she had to look out for herself and put distance between her and this man who was wrong for her in every way—or the man she'd thought was wrong.

Oh, boy. If there was an award to hand out for the world's biggest fool, she'd be receiving the honor right now. Never in a million years would she have expected Matt to make a sacrifice like this for her, and now that he had, she felt ashamed for not giving him more credit.

"Problem is," Brayton went on, "even if Matt insists on stepping down, you're not getting his job."

"What?" Matt argued. "You told me weeks ago she was your toss-up."

Hall grabbed a pencil and began tapping it against the arm of his chair. "And since then I've decided she's not right for the position."

Matt began to rise from his chair, that gratified expression quickly giving way to anger, but Brayton held up a hand. "Matt, you're the best candidate to head up the new team. It's as simple as that. But that doesn't mean I didn't have plans for Carly." The man huffed and shook his head. "Honestly, if I'd known promoting you first was going to cause all this commotion, I would have waited and handled you both together."

Matt slowly returned to his seat, but his eyes remained cautious and distrustful.

"Carly," Brayton said, turning his gaze to hers. "I want to organize a new training unit. I can't think of a better person to head it up."

"Now, wait a minute—" Matt started.

Carly slapped a hand to his thigh. "I'm listening."

"You'd start off taking Renee and Andrea, along with Human Resources and Payroll. I want it combined with a new unit to look after training and staff development. We can negotiate what we call the new department, but in short, you'll be the person taking care of this place, handling pay and benefits, employee relations and continuing education."

She looked at Matt, then back to Mr. Hall. "I don't have much training in employment law. That's a very specialized field."

"Trust me, you're a natural. We'll get you the schooling you need, and your programming background will keep you in touch with the needs of the staff."

A smile began to form on her face. She had to admit the job sounded exciting. She loved working with people, which was why she'd been so anxious to head up the new development team. It had been more about wanting to build the team environment than actually developing Web sites, and as Mr. Hall's ideas began to buzz through her mind, she got more and more excited.

"What about pay?" Matt asked, not nearly as enthused as Carly.

Hall gave them an exasperated look. "I'll pay her exactly what I'm paying you and she can have the office next to yours. Will that make you two happy?"

Matt turned his eyes to Carly, who responded by grinning widely.

"I sort of like maple better than mahogany," she said. Hall raised a brow. "And if I need to get an associate degree in Human Resources, I'll want time off to study."

Matt eyed her proudly while Hall's pencil tapping accelerated.

"I can go along with all this if you accept Carly's counteroffer," Matt urged.

"Under two conditions," Hall said. "One, if there's going to be any hanky-panky between you two, stay out of my lab."

Carly's cheeks enflamed.

"And two, if you have any more lover's quarrels, they better be off my campus."

Matt beamed. "We can do that."

Hall tossed the pencil on his desk. "So is everyone happy?"

They nodded.

"No one's quitting and no one's stepping down?"

They shook their heads.

"Good. Then maybe everyone can get back to work." He rose from his desk and shook both their hands. "Carly, your new job is effective immediately." Then he winked. "I'll see what I can do about your furniture."

"Thank you," she grinned, and without a moment's hesitation Matt pulled her out of the office.

The two scampered down the hall and into Matt's office, where he closed the door, pressed her against it and covered her mouth with his.

"I love you, babe," he whispered in her mouth, then he pressed a trail of eager kisses down her neck, and Carly's heart swelled.

"You were really going to step down for me?"

He tugged the shoulder off her sleeveless tank and replaced it with his lips. "I needed to prove to you I'm not the jerk who filled out that survey."

"You chose me over your job."

He stopped kissing her shoulder and looked into her eyes without a shred of doubt in his gaze. "Baby, I'd choose you over my life. I'm in love with you. I'll do whatever I have to do to prove it to you."

A lump lodged in her throat, leaving her speechless and teary. Instead of waiting for a response, he simply kissed her deeply, circling her tongue with his and pressing his stiff erection against her waist. She sank against him, her heart aching to drink him in and soak up every ounce of love and affection he was offering.

"I'm sorry I doubted you," she whispered. "Do you forgive me?"

"Only if you love me back."

She wrapped her arms around his neck and squeezed him tightly. "I'll love you forever with all my heart."

"Then, yes, I forgive you," he said, slipping his hands up under her shirt.

She kissed his chin, then nibbled a path to his ear. "Hall said no hanky-panky."

"He said to stay out of the lab."

She giggled. "I think that was just a figure of speech."

He cupped her breasts and squeezed a gasp from her chest, devouring the tender flesh of her neck as he worked to get under her clothes. The man was ravenous, his hands licking flames with every deep caress, and as heat pooled at the apex of her thighs she quickly lost the will to fight it.

"Then, as the new Training and Development Manager, you'll have to give me a few lessons on how to interpret instructions," he said. "I'm not very good at it."

And when he reached up under her skirt and got himself under her panties, he proved how very bad he was.

Epilogue

"HERE YOU GO, MRS. Jacobs. It's the last remnant of pink on this house, and I think you deserve the honor of extinguishing it."

Matt handed Carly the brush and the can of gray-green paint the store had named "Suede." They'd remodeled the entire house, bringing it twenty-five years into the present, the 1980s style finally sent to that decor graveyard along with brass trim, big hair and fat shoulder pads.

Holding the brush in her hand, she walked up the path that was now spotted with creamy white kitty paws, Mr. Doodles having thought nothing of walking across a paint lid and leaving his tracks up the walk. Matt and Carly had decided not to wash it off, the prints good warning to visitors who dare come inside.

He was such a bad cat.

As Matt mocked a trumpet playing "Taps," Carly covered over the pink paint, leaving her beautiful little bungalow fully restored and ready for the twenty-first century.

She stepped back down the path and cloaked herself in Matt's arms as they stood on the driveway and admired the view.

The antique tea roses still lined the path, but they'd excavated and replaced the borders with a more earthy covering of shredded redwood. Now, walking up the path, the air was filled with the woodsy scent and the sweet fragrance of roses, the paw prints adding a touch of whimsy in the newly land-scaped garden.

Keeping in tune with the neighborhood, they'd mounted a decorative flag next to the garage door. This one appropriately displayed a merry Santa, now that Thanksgiving was over and they were heading toward Christmas.

The flag across the street still honored the faded remnants of Halloween.

The two stood and admired the view. "It's gone. All the pink is really gone."

"Well, it took almost a year, but it was worth it. According to Josie down the street, you'll make a hefty profit on this house."

"*We'll* make a hefty profit," she corrected, bending down to place the lid on the can and the brush on top of it. "Remember, this is *our* house now, and I'd like to enjoy it for a while before we look for something bigger."

He placed a hand over her belly, just barely beginning to swell with their first child. "I say we've got a year or two before the family outgrows it."

Carly smiled and kissed him, trying to remember a time in her life when she'd dared to dream she could be this happy. There was a time she feared she'd have to choose between a dull and steady man or a wild, sexy bad boy who kept the bed-sheets burning. In Matt she had both, and she'd forever be thankful for the precious gift she'd been given.

While Carly's mother was still content with her part-time husband, Carly had found love in all its perfection.

A car horn sounded behind them.

"I kinda miss the pink," Adam yelled from the driver's seat of his Ford Mustang.

"You would," Matt replied. "It fit your personality, *sweetheart.*"

Adam laughed. "So are you ready or what?"

Matt was heading for the batting cages, having decided to join Adam's softball team in the spring, and no one was happier than Adam. Matt would be their ringer, the man who would win them a championship, he believed. Carly was glad he'd finally put the past behind him. His baseball days were no longer a sour source of resentment but held only fond memories of a chapter in his life he now looked back on with pride.

He'd become a regular batting coach at the Dugout, offering free lessons to kids whose families couldn't afford the standard fees, and Matt relished the gift of giving back, throwing attention at boys much like himself who often came from troubled homes and needed the sympathetic ear of someone who understood.

Stu Callebrew had been dropping hints that he could use a partner for the Dugout, and Matt was considering it as an option if he chose to retire from Web design some day.

First he needed to make enough money to buy Stu some new machines.

Picking up the paint can and brush, Matt called over his shoulder, "Give me a second to grab my bag."

Carly followed him into the house, stopping him in her new wood-floored entryway to wrap her arms around him and give him a kiss.

"I love you," she said.

He kissed her deep and slow. "I love you back."

Stu had said, *Life has a way of fixing things.* And it was true. They'd both been on a path in search of love and stability, each heading in the wrong direction until life slammed them together against their will. It had forced them to see what was right in front of them, what two stubborn and bullheaded Web designers had kept trying to ignore.

Life has a way of fixing things.

Matt and Carly Jacobs would forever be thankful for that.

* * * * *

Look for LAST WOLF WATCHING
by Rhyannon Byrd—the exciting conclusion in the
BLOODRUNNERS miniseries from Silhouette Nocturne.

Follow Michaela and Brody on their fierce journey
to find the truth and face the demons from the past,
as they reach the heart of the battle between
the Runners and the rogues.

Here is a sneak preview of book three,
LAST WOLF WATCHING.

Michaela squinted, struggling to see through the impenetrable darkness. Everyone looked toward the Elders, but she knew Brody Carter still watched her. Michaela could feel the power of his gaze. Its heat. Its strength. And something that felt strangely like anger, though he had no reason to have any emotion toward her. Strangers from different worlds, brought together beneath the heavy silver moon on a night made for hell itself. That was their only connection.

The second she finished that thought, she knew it was a lie. But she couldn't deal with it now. Not tonight. Not when her whole world balanced on the edge of destruction.

Willing her backbone to keep her upright, Michaela Doucet focused on the towering blaze of a roaring bonfire that rose from the far side of the clearing, its orange flames burning with maniacal zeal against the inky black curtain of the night.

Many of the Lycans had already shifted into their preternatural shapes, their fur-covered bodies standing like monstrous shadows at the edges of the forest as they waited with restless expectancy for her brother.

Her nineteen-year-old brother, Max, had been attacked by a rogue werewolf—a Lycan who preyed upon humans for food. Max had been bitten in the attack, which meant he was no longer human, but a breed of creature that existed between the two worlds of man and beast, much like the Bloodrunners themselves.

The Elders parted, and two hulking shapes emerged from the trees. In their wolf forms, the Lycans stood over seven feet tall, their legs bent at an odd angle as they stalked forward. They each held a thick chain that had been wound around their inside wrists, the twin lengths leading back into the shadows. The Lycans had taken no more than a few steps when they jerked on the chains, and her brother appeared.

Bound like an animal.

Biting at her trembling lower lip, she glanced left, then right, surprised to see that others had joined her. Now the Bloodrunners and their family and friends stood as a united force against the Silvercrest pack, which had yet to accept the fact that something sinister was eating away at its foundation—something that would rip down the protective walls that separated their world from the humans'. It occurred to Michaela that loyalties were being announced tonight—a separation made between those who would stand with the Runners in their fight against the rogues and those who blindly supported the pack's refusal to face reality. But all she could focus on was her brother. Max looked so hurt…so terrified.

"Leave him alone," she screamed, her soft-soled, black

satin slip-ons struggling for purchase in the damp earth as she rushed toward Max, only to find herself lifted off the ground when a hard, heavily muscled arm clamped around her waist from behind, pulling her clear off her feet. "Damn it, let me down!" she snarled, unable to take her eyes off her brother as the golden-eyed Lycan kicked him.

Mindless with heartache and rage, Michaela clawed at the arm holding her, kicking her heels against whatever part of her captor's legs she could reach. "Stop it," a deep, husky voice grunted in her ear. "You're not helping him by losing it. I give you my word he'll survive the ceremony, but you have to keep it together."

"Nooooo!" she screamed, too hysterical to listen to reason. "You're monsters! All of you! Look what you've done to him! How dare you! *How dare you!*"

The arm tightened with a powerful flex of muscle, cinching her waist. Her breath sucked in on a sharp, wailing gasp.

"Shut up before you get both yourself and your brother killed. I will *not* let that happen. Do you understand me?" her captor growled, shaking her so hard that her teeth clicked together. "Do you understand me, Doucet?"

"Damn it," she cried, stricken as she watched one of the guards grab Max by his hair. Around them Lycans huffed and growled as they watched the spectacle, while others outright howled for the show to begin.

"That's enough!" the voice seethed in her ear. "They'll tear you apart before you even reach him, and I'll be damned if I'm going to stand here and watch you die."

Suddenly, through the haze of fear and agony and outrage in her mind, she finally recognized who'd caught her. *Brody.*

He held her in his arms, her body locked against his powerful form, her back to the burning heat of his chest. A low, keening sound of anguish tore through her, and her head dropped forward as hoarse sobs of pain ripped from her throat. "Let me go. I have to help him. *Please,*" she begged brokenly, knowing only that she needed to get to Max. "Let me go, Brody."

He muttered something against her hair, his breath warm against her scalp, and Michaela could have sworn it was a single word…. But she must have heard wrong. She was too upset. Too furious. Too terrified. She must be out of her mind.

Because it sounded as if he'd quietly snarled the word *never.*

nocturne™

THE FINAL INSTALLMENT OF
THE BLOODRUNNERS TRILOGY

Last Wolf Watching

Runner Brody Carter has found his match in
Michaela Doucet, a human with unusual psychic powers.
When Michaela's brother is threatened, Brody becomes
her protector, and suddenly not only has to protect her
from her enemies but also from himself....

LOOK FOR
LAST WOLF WATCHING
BY
RHYANNON
BYRD

Available May 2008 wherever you buy books.

Dramatic and Sensual Tales of Paranormal Romance

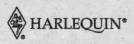
HARLEQUIN®

American ★ *Romance*®

Three Boys and a Baby

When Ella Garvey's eight-year-old twins and
their best friend, Dillon, discover an abandoned
baby girl, they fear she will be put in jail—
or worse! They decide to take matters into their
own hands and run away. Luckily the outlaws are
found quickly…and Ella finds a second chance
at love—with Dillon's dad, Jackson.

LOOK FOR

Three Boys and a Baby

BY

LAURA MARIE ALTOM

*Available May
wherever you buy books.*

LOVE, HOME & HAPPINESS

SPECIAL EDITION™

 THE WILDER FAMILY
Healing Hearts in Walnut River

Social worker Isobel Suarez was proud to
work at Walnut River General Hospital, so
when Neil Kane showed up from the attorney
general's office to investigate insurance fraud,
she was up in arms. Until she melted in his
arms, and things got very tricky...

Look for

HER MR. RIGHT?

by

KAREN ROSE SMITH

Available May wherever books are sold.

REQUEST YOUR FREE BOOKS!

2 FREE NOVELS PLUS 2 FREE GIFTS!

HARLEQUIN® Blaze™

Red-hot reads!

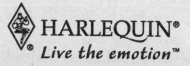

Romantic
SUSPENSE

Sparked by Danger,
Fueled by Passion.

Seduction Summer:
Seduction in the sand...and a killer on the beach.

Silhouette Romantic Suspense invites you to the hottest
summer yet with three connected stories from some
of our steamiest storytellers! Get ready for...

Killer Temptation
by Nina Bruhns;
a millionaire this tempting is worth a little danger.

Killer Passion
by Sheri WhiteFeather;
an FBI profiler's forbidden passion incites a
killer's rage,

and

Killer Affair
by Cindy Dees;
this affair with a mystery man is to die for.

Look for

KILLER TEMPTATION by Nina Bruhns in June 2008
KILLER PASSION by Sheri WhiteFeather in July 2008
and
KILLER AFFAIR by Cindy Dees in August 2008.

Available wherever you buy books!

COMING NEXT MONTH

#393 INDULGE ME Isabel Sharpe
Forbidden Fantasies
Darcy Wolf has three wild fantasies she's going to fulfill before she leaves town.
But after seducing her hottie housepainter Tyler Houston, she might just have
to put Fantasy #2 and Fantasy #3 on hold!

#394 NIGHTCAP Kathleen O'Reilly
Those Sexy O'Sullivans, Bk. 3
Sean O'Sullivan—watch out! Three former college girlfriends have just hatched
a revenge plot on the world's most lovable womanizer. Cleo Hollings, in
particular, is anxious to get started on her make-life-difficult-for-Sean plan.
Only, she never guesses how difficult it will be for her when she starts sleeping
with the enemy.

#395 UP CLOSE AND PERSONAL Joanne Rock
Who's impersonating sizzling sensuality guru Jessica Winslow? Rocco Easton is
going undercover to find out. And he has to do it soon, because the identity thief
is getting braver, pretending to be Jessica everywhere—even in his bed!

#396 A SEXY TIME OF IT Cara Summers
Extreme
Bookstore owner Neely Rafferty can't believe it when she realizes that the time-
traveling she does in her dreams is actually real. And so, she soon discovers,
is the sexy time-cop who's come to stop her. Max Gale arrives in 2008 with a
job to do. And he'll do it, too—if Neely ever lets him out of her bed....

#397 FIRE IN THE BLOOD Kelley St. John
The Sixth Sense, Bk. 4
Chantalle Bedeau is being haunted by a particularly nasty ghost, and the only
person who can help her is medium Tristan Vicknair. Sure, she hasn't seen him
since their incredible one-night stand but what's the worst he can do—give her
the best sex of her life again?

#398 HAVE MERCY Jo Leigh
Do Not Disturb
Pet concierge Mercy Jones has seen it all working at the exclusive Hush Hotel
in Manhattan. But when sexy Will Desmond saunters in with his pooch she's
shocked by the fantasies he generates. This is one man who could unleash the
animal in Mercy!

HBCNM0408